THE GO-BETWEEN

THE GO-BETWEEN

VERONICA CHAMBERS

DELACORTE PRESS

Text copyright © 2017 by Veronica Chambers
Jacket art copyright © 2017 by Kelly Blair

Visit us on the Web! randomhouseteens.com

Educators and librarians, for a variety of teaching tools, visit us at RHTeachersLibrarians.com

Library of Congress Cataloging-in-Publication Data is available upon request.
ISBN 978-1-101-93095-3 (hc) — ISBN 978-1-101-93096-0 (ebook)
ISBN 978-1-5247-6476-0 (intl. tr. pbk.)

The text of this book is set in 12-point Electra LH.
Interior design by Ken Crossland

Printed in the United States of America
10 9 8 7 6 5 4 3 2 1
First Edition

For Flora
No pares, sigue, sigue

Welcome to America, but . . .

Everything changes when you move to a new country. Doctors become cabdrivers. Lawyers become waiters.

I'd better clarify.

My mom was once a glamorous TV star in Mexico. She was disappointed to find that her big American debut would feature her playing a Beverly Hills maid. (No sequins, hair extensions, or costume changes required.) True, ours is not the usual immigrant story. We came in as visitors who might want to stay. We are one of the lucky families, but it wasn't all roses for us either.

More than one million immigrants come to the United States each year. Half of them, like me, come from Latin America. (Twenty percent come from Asia, and the other thirty percent come from more than a hundred countries around the globe.) What unites us is that we all have a dream. Before the end of the school year in my new American school, I thought I wanted to go back home. It was, I would learn, a common wish. But life offers so many surprises, and it's not always easy to know the best way to make a dream come true. Can your heart and loyalties be in two places? A dream can change. Take my family's situation, for example.

PART ONE

Mexico City

1

A MEXICAN FAIRY TALE

My mother, María Carolina Josefina del Valle y Calderón, was cast in her first telenovela when she was just a couple of years older than I am now. She was eighteen when she was cast as Bianca in *Mundos sin Fronteras*, a telenovela about a mission in Alta California in the early 1800s. In the series, she aged twenty years in twelve months. Viewers loved the story of a poor Mexican woman who moves to Alta California, the northernmost region of California when it was still part of Mexico and considered the Wild, Wild West. In those times, and in the TV show, because the region was so sparsely populated, women were allowed to own property, and a handful became very rich. My mother's character evolved over the course of the telenovela from a humble but drop-dead-gorgeous (of course) cattle hand to the wife of an older, cold, and abusive ranch owner, and then to an independent widow who runs a prosperous business. Finally, in her thirties, she married for love. Do I sound like I know the whole thing by heart? Does it sound predictable? Who cares. My mom was a hit. I've seen it about thirty times.

Mexican TV viewers have always loved this genre of telenovela, *romance histórico,* or historical romance. But *Mundos sin Fronteras* became—unintentionally, my mother says—a feminist touch point, igniting a spirit of independence in women that was unprecedented. Millions of viewers tuned in to watch the show, and from the first episode until the last, the series set ratings records that are unbroken to this day.

When my mother got depressed—although not often, it was still, for me, too often—she lay on the couch and watched videos of Princess Diana. Cocooned in her favorite silk robe, my mother, Carolina, started off with the Charles and Diana wedding video. It was a video I'd seen so often, I could recite the archbishop of Canterbury's lines by heart: "Here is the stuff of which fairy tales are made. The prince and princess on their wedding day." Then she cycled through Diana's life, the fashion evolution and the red carpet, her meeting with Michael Jackson, her friendship with Elton John. She was bawling by the time Diana became a mother the first time, then the second time.

At this point, because my mother had called in sick, the phone was ringing off the hook. But my mother wouldn't be distracted by such pettiness, because now we were deep into the footage of Diana the activist. By the time we got to Diana the land mines activist, my mother had dried her tears. It was a catharsis, this viewing, and like Diana, my mother had put aside her grief and private heartbreaks in search of something more meaningful.

What chilled me, and my father, and my brother when he is back home, was the last round of videos. It was always an array of videos about Princess Diana and the paparazzi, leading to Diana's tragic death. I didn't know anyone who'd ever ridden in a car with a celebrity while SUVs filled with photographers and TV crews raced you down a highway and through tunnels who could watch that footage and not feel the fear. It was like a police chase on steroids, all for a stupid photo.

For as long as I could remember, people had been taking my mother's picture. It tapered off over time. I was very young when she first became truly famous, and sometimes it seemed more like a movie I saw than something I lived, the little girl turning in to the folds of her mother's dress so that the cameras that *pop, pop, pop*ped with their lights and their long lenses didn't get a picture of her face. There used to be dozens of photographers at all times back then, and sometimes when my mother went out shopping or to lunch with a friend, they would surround the car so that it couldn't move. Even after my father hired full-time security, a guard for each of us, the paparazzi were always there yelling to my mother: "*Bella, bella, guapa, guapa, mira aquí.*" Beautiful. Gorgeous. Look over here.

When she wasn't sad and feeling a kinship to the Princess of Wales, my mother told us stories about how early on, when she first became famous, she allowed her relatives to sell "exclusives" to the tabloids. "That's how all my *primos* bought their houses," she said. "If those papers are going to make money off me, then it's only right that *mi gente* gets to eat too."

My mother had been famous for so long that photos of her were no longer such a "get." There were, however, always four or five stalwarts staked out at our house and at the studio where my mother shot her *novelas*. The minute our huge black car rolled down the long driveway and the giant gates that stood like sentinels opened, you could hear the photographers—the clicks of their cameras rapid like machine guns.

Now everyone had a camera in their phone, which meant it wasn't just the pros who grabbed photos of my mother. When we went out to a restaurant, you could see the people who were pretending to be looking at their phone but were actually snapping her pic.

What this meant was that my mother had to be camera ready at all times. Her glam squad—Andy, who did her hair, and Regina, who did her makeup—practically lived at our house.

I loved them. Andy not only did hair, but he made the most amazing jewelry. He made a necklace for my *quinceañera*. It was a gold disc meant to be the moon, with my star sign drawn in tiny diamond specks. Regina was a great person. I loved her impression of my mom!

The thing about telenovela culture was, it was all about bigger is better. Shoulder-length hair wasn't good enough. Your hair had to be Rapunzel-long, for when the wind machines got going. It was ultra-dramatic. The dresses were tight, the heels were high, and the makeup was two ticks away from being drag-queen-worthy. My mom did it well. She was considered the best telenovela actress in Mexico because no one could out-bombshell her.

For me, my mother without makeup was . . . beautiful. It was like she was a superhero in reverse. Her beauty was only revealed when she took the mask off.

But as famous as my mom was, the person I always worshipped is my father, Reinaldo. It didn't hurt that he voiced Buzz Lightyear in the Spanish-language version of *Toy Story*. He did the job years before I was born, one of his first big breaks. But when I was a kid, the movie seemed to me entirely brand-new and as larger-than-life as its makers intended. I remember at five or six being genuinely shocked that the voice that grumbled *"Buenos días"* to me each morning and told me bedtime stories each night was also on my TV. I wondered how it could be that my father was a superhero toy astronaut who came to life the minute all the kids left the room. For a year, I insisted he whisper *"Al infinito . . . y más allá!"*—"To infinity . . . and beyond!"—to me instead of the typical *"sueños dulces"* or "sweet dreams." And in first grade, for my mother's annual Día de los Muertos party, my father dressed up as Buzz Lightyear. I was dressed up as Jessie, with a costume handmade by the best seamstresses at TexCoco, the big studio in Mexico City where my

7

mother shot all her telenovelas. I also had a bright red wig made of real human hair, fashioned by my mother's favorite wigmaker.

My parents were good at their jobs, so we lived in this amazing house — ten bedrooms, fourteen bathrooms, a pool, a tennis court, a guesthouse, a greenhouse, the works. We also had a massive staff. There was Alberta, who we called Albita, our live-in housekeeper, who had been with our family since I was a baby. Albita was tall and thin, with long black hair that she wore wrapped on the top of her head in a ballet bun. She didn't actually clean our house; she was more like the house manager. There were Irma and Cristina, who did most of the cleaning and shopping.

Diana was my mother's yoga teacher, who doubled as an organic chef. She cooked all my mother's lunches, and her dinner too when my mother was on a diet, which was any day that ended in a *y*. My father liked more traditional Mexican meals that Albita made herself.

Albita used to be a high school track star. My older brother, Sergio, always said Alberta was too fit to be just a housekeeper. He thought she was undercover security. There were three guys who worked as our official security and drivers. In Mexico, if you've got money, kidnapping is always a fear. Every year, hundreds of people in Mexico are kidnapped for ransom. Sometimes even when the families pay, the kidnappers kill the captured person anyway. I didn't know anyone who had been kidnapped, but Sergio did. As did my parents, though they rarely talked about it. I grew up just knowing that it could happen and that our drivers were more than security; they were our lifelines. They lived in an apartment above the garage, and they took turns sleeping in the guest bedroom on the first floor of our house. We were never alone.

So Raul—tall, ripped, with a neck the size of a tree trunk—guarded my mother and drove her wherever she needed to go. Juan Manuel, a former martial arts champ, drove my father to his sets and gave Papá lessons in everything from kickboxing to kali, the art of stick fighting. My guy was Samir; he was young and good-looking. He could've been a telenovela star himself. He drove me back and forth to school in a bulletproof car.

"You should be on TV," I would tell him, trying to flirt. "You should quit this job and become an actor."

He would laugh and say, "To be an actor, I'd have to have talent."

I'd shrug and insist, "You could take lessons. I bet the camera would love you."

He'd shake his head and say, "No way, Camilla. I'm too shy." And then he'd turn to driving. My heart would melt in ten seconds flat like a cupcake that you put in a microwave too long. I mean, is there anything better, sweeter, than a guy who looks like a prince who tells you that he is shy? But obviously he knew, as I did, that he was a member of my parents' staff and only that.

Sometimes after school when Samir drove me to the mall so I could shop and hang out with my friends, I would beg him to let me sit in the front, next to him. He never allowed it.

"I've got protocols, Camilla," he would say, shaking his head.

Sergio once saw me flirting with Samir and warned me to stop. "You think it's a game," he said. "But this is his livelihood. If Mom or Dad thought that any of the staff were behaving inappropriately, they'd be fired—without any references. You'd not only make him lose his job, but hurt his ability to find another. So go flirt with one of those pencil-neck losers at your school, Cammi. Pick on someone your own age."

Even when I don't like to hear it, Sergio is my moral conscience. He's the best thing that ever happened to this family, and we all agree—my mother, my father, and me. I'm not being sarcastic. Some people are so good that they almost seem to have a halo above their head. That's Sergio. My mother said that before I was born, she thought he would become a vet because every wounded animal Sergio could find, from three-legged cats to birds with broken wings, were brought home for him to tend and heal.

My father said that by junior high school, Sergio was such a devoted reader of the Bible and other religious texts that my father thought he might become a priest or a religious scholar. Sergio was patient with me, until I got older—I could see him trying to mold my mind.

"Mama, you should buy her books that make her think. Her brain will atrophy," Sergio pleaded with my mother one time.

"When I was her age . . . ," my mother began.

Sergio smiled and said, "I know, Mama. There was no

money for books or anything else. We know how lucky we are. Could you please let me order some reading for her?"

My mother reached into her purse and handed my brother a credit card. "Order some books online. And no pornos for yourself. I will be watching the bills."

Andy and Regina laughed as my brother blushed. But he took the card and kissed my mother on the cheek, and just a few days later, the treats began to arrive. *The Secret Garden. Little Women.* And my favorite, the Nancy Drew series. It was like Christmas had come early. From the age of eight, I fell in love with detective stories, and I knew that while my parents loved me, my brother was my guardian angel. He saw me and looked out for me in ways that nobody else did. It was like I was one of those little creatures in his pet hospital. He would not let harm come to me before I could fly on my own.

The year I turned ten, Sergio went away to boarding school in England. It was, my parents explained, at his teachers' behest. Even the best schools in Mexico City were not challenging enough for my big brother. He was, at sixteen, already fluent in Spanish, English, and French. A good English boarding school would set him up for a good European university, and that, my father explained, would set Sergio up for life. I cried for days before he left, and even though he reassured me again and again "I am always with you" and tried to get me to read science fiction books about teleportation, I didn't believe him and didn't care. I was convinced the world was a dark place without Sergio nearby, and in some ways, everything I will tell you and everything that happens boils down to this. I am now sixteen, exactly the age Sergio was when he went away to school. I understand that he had to go. I stand here, on the brink of my own big leap; I am sympathetic to how scary it must have been to start a new life in a new country. But let me tell you a little bit more about the past before I get to the present.

Sergio excelled at boarding school, picking up German as a fourth language. The first Christmas he came back, he gave me the Harry Potter books translated into Spanish, and it helped me to think of him—dark-haired and bespectacled just like that wizard—learning magic and playing Quidditch in that faraway place. Sergio went to college at Oxford, and now he's twenty-two, in business school in Switzerland. I imagine sometimes that the business school is just a cover and that Sergio is really a spy, a Mexican James Bond, tooling around the Swiss Alps in a sporty silver two-seater, fighting bad guys and romancing beautiful ladies.

2

★

#RKOMC

The kids I grew up with are easily understood if you check out a scandalous Instagram account called #RKOMC— Rich Kids of Mexico City. It started out in Spanish, *los chicos ricos de Mexico*, but then the phenomenon went global. Four hundred thousand followers on Instagram, and now it's all in English so everyone can know how these kids roll. It's not uncommon for them to keep exotic animals, such as lions and tigers, as pets in their families' sprawling country mansions. It's illegal, and in any other country the animals would be confiscated and the owners would face charges, but in Mexico you can be sixteen and post a picture of yourself with a baby jaguar, and it'll go on Instagram and get a thousand likes. As tacky as it is, the kids—kids I go to school with—will post photos of piles of cash with a tag that says, *"haciendo un poco de compras."* There are lots of photos of boys and girls tagged *"con mi Black."* It's not as racist as it sounds. *Mi Black* is a nickname for an American Express black card. Vacation photos were a must—especially if it involved a private plane or a yacht. And if the view was stunning, you could count on it being tagged along the lines of *"esta vista no es para cualquiera"*—this view is not for everyone.

The Rich Kids of Mexico City is, of course, Sergio's worst nightmare, but it's also like a car wreck from which he cannot turn away. "Did you see the latest?" he says whenever he calls. "Some tool posted a photo of his arm on the stick shift of a Ferrari, with three Bulgari watches on. This in a country where the average national income is fourteen thousand dollars a year, for a large family. But there are the super/mega-rich, just much less than the one percent in the US. Where is the respect?"

If you're above the age of twenty-one, then you call these spoiled kids "Juniors," since the money they are spending is always from their parents, never anything they actually earned. True, I am technically one of this shameful cohort, but thanks to my brother's influence, you'll never see a scandalous photo of me online.

The #RKOMC crew likes to refer to themselves as "Mireyes," which sounds like a family name but really stands for *"mi reyes,"* or "my kings." And lest you think that it's all for show and that the pictures, though in poor taste, are meaningless, you should see how the Mireyes flex their influence offline. One of these princesses famously showed up for Sunday brunch at Misol-Ha, one of the top restaurants in the city. She then proceeded to throw a fit when they wouldn't seat her and her friends without a reservation. It just so happened that her father ran the government agency that does health inspections. Within twenty-four hours, the restaurant had been shut down.

My friend Patrizia, much to Sergio's annoyance, made frequent appearances on #RKOMC. She's an old-school rich girl—her dad owns a whole construction empire, so she's seen it all before—the big house, the fancy cars, the bodyguards, and the bling. I used to try to be friends with the nicer, less vulgar girls at school, but it was always the same thing. Whenever they came over to my house, they'd ask my mother for autographs. "Not for me," they'd insist. *"Por mi madre/tia/abuela."* For their moms. Aunts. Grandmothers. Whatever.

It's one of my rules: you can't be my friend if you ask my mother for an autograph. You can't be my friend if you take a selfie with my mom. You can't be my friend if you post a picture of my house on Instagram or tweet, "OMG. Hanging @ casa de @CarolinaDV #pinchme." You may be a nice girl. You may have an Einstein brain and a heart of gold. But it doesn't work for me—fandom. Every year, ever since I was old enough to arrange my own playdates, I tried to make new friends. But they always broke one, if not several, of my rules.

In fourth grade, I became close with Eva Jiminez. Eva was a quiet girl with dark hair and big round glasses, kind of like a Latina Hermione Granger. I met her in gymnastics class and we used to talk about how cool it would be to represent Mexico in the Olympics. The truth was that the only thing I was ever really good at was the floor routines, but Eva had mad skills: she was a somersaulting, flipping machine. Imagine how embarrassed I was when, at my ninth birthday party, she announced that she was "dedicating a performance to Cammi and her super-talented mother." She began flipping around the living room and broke my mother's favorite vase. My mother didn't mind. "People first, things second," she always said. But I was mortified. It was like watching someone audition for one of those reality shows. The way she stomped around the room and flipped and flipped and flipped, it seemed like she was hoping that maybe a casting director was in the room and she might be "discovered."

Sergio said that I was being ungenerous, that after all, she had said she was dedicating her performance to me and my mom. But then Eva came running over to us and whispered, "Do you think any of the producers from your mother's show are here at the party? Wouldn't it be great if they did a telenovela about a talented little gymnast and your mother could play my mom?" It was hard enough for me sometimes to accept that my mother loved me and Sergio above all, that she wasn't just "playing my mom" when she came home from work. I didn't want to, I just couldn't be friends with girls who thought that having an actress as a mother was a total fantasy.

In fifth grade, Laura Garcia, who shared my love of making comecocos, or fortune-tellers, was my best friend. The first time she visited our home, she spent the whole time asking my mother for autographs. "Not for me," she said. "But for my mother and my aunt, and my neighbor and the lady who runs the restaurant down the street, who are *all* your biggest fans." At our next playdate, she brought both her mother and her aunt, who spent the entire time in the kitchen, quizzing Albita about my mother's favorite meals and workout habits.

No matter how hard I tried to explain, they never seemed to get how many hours my mother worked, how surreal it was sometimes to turn on the TV or open a magazine and see her there. It was easier for Sergio, I think. One because he was a genius and he had this way of figuring things — even the tough, confusing, life things — out. But he was also a boy and no one ever *compared* him to our mother. My parents did their best to keep me out of the press, but reporters still managed to find the dorkiest school pictures of me and run them with cruel captions like

DNA DISASTER:
Carolina sobs, "She is a brain, but no beauty."

Patrizia may be an imperious spoiled brat, but she doesn't ooh and aah around my family, and she gets points for that. Patrizia was fond of saying, "I may be a bitch, but I'm *your* bitch, Cammi," and I took it to mean that no matter what, she had my back.

As for Patrizia's appearances on #RKOMC, I'd say they

were respectably tame. Most of the photos were of her out and about in the city, looking just a little like Audrey Hepburn in her oversized shades and giving *abrazos* to Che, her adorable little pug. Che even had his own Instagram account with more than a thousand followers—@jajaconcheche. "*Ja*" means "ha-ha" in English, but people in Mexico use it the way Americans use "LOL."

One night, Patrizia invited me to a club in Coyoacán. I hardly ever go to clubs. I'm sixteen, which means that while girls my age can get in, most of the guys can't. House parties, especially since all the houses have pools, are way more popular. But Coyoacán is an old colonial village, about twenty minutes south of the city. Its name means "place of the coyotes" or "place of the wells," depending on who you ask, and it was once the seat of the Aztec empire. It's where the Tepanec chief first welcomed the Spanish conquistadores, and where Cortes began his assault on the Aztec empire. It's where Leon Trotsky lived and was murdered by Stalin's agents, and where Frida Kahlo fell in love with Diego Rivera. It was the home of the great Mexican poet Octavio Paz and the oh-so-elegant queen of Mexican cinema, Dolores Del Rio. It's still the place where writers and artists and actors like to live, and if my mother had not become so famous, it's where my father said we would have lived too. When I was little, I used to imagine an alternate universe where we lived in a little Moroccan-style casita and my parents acted in local productions of classic plays. We don't go to Coyoacán often, but it's one of my absolute favorite places to hang out.

Mexico City during the day can be like a hundred-degree hurricane: too hot, too many people, moving too fast through this vortex of time and space. But at night, the city cools down and slows down, especially on the weekends. My father said I could go out with Patrizia as long as Samir drove us and came along to chaperone, which was fine with me. I'd never known anyone who had been kidnapped, but we read about the kidnappings every day. Having Samir along made me feel safe, like nothing bad was going to happen.

From the moment we piled into the black SUV, I was excited. As we rolled past the city limits, I cracked the windows and stared out at the stars peeking through the jacaranda trees, in their full, show-offy purple bloom. When we arrived in Coyoacán, it was still a little early to hit the club. The sun had barely set, so we decided to walk through the plazas. I love to see all the stalls where the artists have set up their work. There are a hundred copycats of the region's most famous residents, so many of the paintings are done *en el estilo de Frida o como Diego*. I, for one, can never resist buying a three-hundred-peso Frida knockoff (around twenty US dollars). I have six in my room already. But when we walked through the stalls, Patrizia insisted on treating me to a copy of one I didn't have yet, *The Two Fridas*.

"*Por mi mejor amiga*," she said, handing the painting to me. For my best friend.

I gave her a hug. I was genuinely touched.

After we put the painting in the car, I would have been

just happy spending the rest of the night walking around the plaza. When I was a kid, we never visited the big outdoor markets like this. We couldn't; my mother would have been bum-rushed. Every once in a while, I would visit Coyoacán or someplace like it with my dad and Sergio, but not so often that I ever got my fill of it.

Walking through the town square, or *zocalo*, I understood why they called this particular part of the city the Barrio Magico. I never felt as deeply Mexican as I did at an open-air street fair. (Well, a professional soccer game was a close second.) Like a kid, I couldn't get enough of the *elotes*, corn on the cob grilled over an open flame, then doused with mayo, lime, chili pepper, and grated cheese.

"Wow, not afraid at all of the carbs," Patrizia said disdainfully after I scarfed my first *elote* down.

"Not at all," I said. Then I ordered another.

I ate the second one more slowly, savoring each bite as we walked toward the club. I loved the range of street performers, from the mimes and the clowns to those break-dancing to reggaeton beats. But what I loved best was the old couples dancing the *bailes folkloricos*. The men in their short-sleeved starched shirts, tucked neatly into their pants. The women were all like aging ballerinas: postures just so, gray hair swept into the most elegant buns, delicate feet clad in the softest leather shoes. Everything in their careful, considered motions seemed to say, "Slow down, slow down." Patrizia, in contrast, made it clear that she needed me to *Apurate, apurate!*

She had scoped out this new nightclub called the Big Bling, and all the cocktails had luxe, metallic touches. But their signature was champagne with twenty-four-karat-gold flecks.

So let's be real. My parents don't want me to drink. But I figured a night out in Coyoacán was a special enough occasion that I could take a few sips of champagne without too much trouble. Especially with Samir there to keep a watchful eye.

The club was on the garden level of this old mansion. You walked through a beautiful ballroom, then down the back steps to the garden, which was landscaped to look like one of those Alice in Wonderland English maze gardens. The paths were lit with fairy lights and torches. It was ah-mazing. Then I saw him.

He was tall and skinny, almost a little too skinny. Except that he was perfect, so on him the skinniness was also perfect. He had black wavy hair that was just a little too long—somewhere between rock-star-cool and long enough for a man bun. He was wearing a white shirt, a tie, a dark vest, and jeans. And this is the thing: when we walked in, he seemed to smile at me as if he knew me.

I was sure that he was smiling at someone else, so I took a quick glance around to see who he might be looking at.

Then he pointed at me.

I was so confused.

I pointed at myself and mouthed, "Me?"

He nodded and mouthed, "Yes. You."

I was so taken aback by the whole interaction that, well, I missed the first step down to the garden. Having bungled that first one, I went tumbling down the other seventeen.

Did I mention that I was wearing a pair of three-inch heels that I had "borrowed" from my mother and that I was absolute crap at walking in? By the time I'd landed at the bottom of the steps, all I could hope was that I'd fallen on some sort of sacred Aztec burial ground and that the earth would open up and swallow me whole.

Samir scooped me up and seated me at a nearby table, but not before Patrizia had snapped a photo of me, lying in a heap, holding on to my mother's shoe with a broken heel as if it might have helped me catch my footing. "For future blackmail purposes," she said, and smirked.

Samir was examining my ankle and said, *"No se, Cammi. Tal vez debo llamar un doctor."*

Then, as if it was one of those crazy-coincidence moments in a telenovela, Handsome to the Point of Distraction showed up and said, *"Soy un doctor. . . .* Well, I'm a medical student at UNAM."

Patrizia whipped around and flashed him one of her Instagram-famous smiles. "I'm Patrizia," she said.

He nodded, then turned to me. "What's your name?"

Patrizia laughed and said, *"Tamila la Torpe."*

"Torpe" means "clumsy" in Spanish, and she knew that when I was little, my brother used to call me *Tamila la Torpe.*

"My name is Camilla," I said, as Handsome examined my swelling ankle.

"I'm Amadeo," he said.

Patrizia bent down and whispered in a faux-sexy voice loud enough for all of us to hear, "Ooooo, Amadeo, I'd like to play doctor with you."

Both Samir and Amadeo looked at her like she was nuts. But I was used to it.

"It doesn't look too bad," Amadeo said, addressing Samir. "But if she can't walk on it tomorrow, she should definitely see a doctor. It might be sprained."

Then he asked Samir, "Hey, man, can I talk to you privately for a second?"

The two of them walked away from us.

"What's that about?" I wondered.

"He's probably gay," Patrizia said dismissively, signaling the waiter.

She ordered two champagnes *"de oro"*—laced with gold—and before Samir and Amadeo returned, our drinks had arrived.

"Compliments of the house," the waiter said, winking at me. "Sorry about your slip."

The wink did not go unnoticed by Patrizia. "What about being clumsy is such a turn-on?" she asked. "You do know that in this friendship, I'm the hot one."

This was something I did know. I was not in any way hot. I lived with one of the most beautiful actresses in the world—my mother. I had no interest in competing on the beauty front. But now it felt strange, strange in a good way, to be out and getting so much attention.

Amadeo and Samir returned, and Amadeo approached me. "Camilla . . . ," he began. *Maldita sea*, how I loved how he said my name.

He handed me his phone, and I punched in the number to my cell.

"I'll call you," he said.

"I'll look forward to it," I said.

"Rest that ankle," he cautioned, smiling. Then he kissed me on the forehead.

Patrizia watched the whole thing with a look of unmitigated confusion that matched the way I felt. Then she gulped down her champagne and drank mine down too. She was about to order another round when Samir said, "Okay, *chicas*, enough. Time to go."

In the car ride home, Patrizia turned belligerent. "I can't believe you would go after Amadeo when you knew I liked him."

I was stunned. We'd met him at the same time. He'd smiled at me first, I thought. But what I said was, "How was I supposed to know that, Patti?"

"You saw me flirting with him!"

I wanted to say that she flirted with everybody. I wanted to explain that I'd spotted him first and that he was kinda sorta the reason I fell. But she was being such a nightmare that I kept my mouth shut.

Samir dropped me off first, and when I got out of the car, I asked Patrizia for my Frida painting, but she wouldn't give it to me.

"No gifts for *vendepatrias*," she said. No gifts for backstabbers.

The next morning when I couldn't stand on my ankle, my mother called our family doctor, Dr. Gomez. She came over, examined my ankle, declared it officially and completely sprained, and ordered me to a weekend of bed rest. I was just trying to decide what I was going to binge-watch on Netflix when my mother's publicist called. She reported that I was on Instagram, the latest brat to be featured on #RKOMC. I grabbed my mother's iPad, and there I was, sprawled on the floor, looking like a mess, clutching the shoe with the broken heel. The tag line read *"Loca en su Louboutins."* It already had 697 likes.

My mother looked at the photo and said, "Wait! Are those my shoes?"

3

★

GLASS HOUSES

Despite her posting my photo to Instagram, Patrizia and I remained friends. I also went out a few times with Amadeo. He was nineteen, premed. My parents thought he was a little old for me, but he was so buttoned-up and responsible that they let me go out with him as long as Samir stayed within shouting distance. My love life, so to speak, was pretty solid. But at home, things were rough.

Back in Mexico, we had this greenhouse. It was as big as some people's houses. There must have been more than five hundred plants in there. The greenhouse was my father's haven, and the rare orchids he collected were his pride. One night, my parents came home from an awards show, and I could tell from the moment the front door opened that my mother had not won any of the awards she had been nominated for. At first there was just peace and the smells I loved. My mother's perfume, the scent of my father—a mixture of cigars and the Bay Rum cologne he liked. Then came the symphony of screams that said all was not well. My mother was cursing in her high soprano voice. My father, his voice big and bold, was uttering assurances and compliments. "You are so beautiful and talented. You know how jealous people are. It's not easy to be a big fish in a small pond. Everybody wants to put a hook in your mouth. This is why we should move to the United States. You need a bigger stage, *cara mia*."

"*Cara mia*" is Italian for "darling." For some, Mexico is a romantic destination. But in Mexico, Italy is a land of allure, and certain phrases, such as "*ciao*" and "*cara mia*," pepper our everyday speech. For those who can afford to, Italy is a favorite destination. Spanish and Italian are close enough that you can travel throughout the country and make your way. The food is divine, and of course the shopping—Gucci, Prada, Dolce & Gabbana—is splendid. We had been going to Italy on vacation for as long as I could remember.

My mother was not soothed by my father's words. She continued to tear through the house—the dining room, the great room, the kitchen—and I could tell by the sounds what she had thrown. In the dining room, she had kicked off her stilettos, then thrown one and then the other at the wooden cabinet that held our fanciest dishes. The big wooden piece had shaken, but from what I could tell, nothing had broken. In the great room, she had grabbed a handful of coasters and now began tossing them, like Frisbees, at the artwork. One was tossed at the Gabriel Orozco; another one was flown at a mural by Minerva Cuevas. The only piece that was never used for target practice was a photograph of Frida Kahlo with a love letter scribbled to one of her many lovers. On the photograph, she wrote, "My Bartoli . . . I don't know how to write love letters. But I wanted to tell you that my whole being opened for you. Since I fell in love with you, everything is transformed and is full of beauty . . . love is like an aroma, like a current, like rain."

In the kitchen my mother paused, then moved on, bypassing the easy pleasure of breaking water glasses and hand-painted ceramic plates. When I heard the door to the garden open, I rushed to the back window so I could see as well as hear the action. It was like a silent movie, the way my mother stomped around barefoot, her duchesse satin ball gown dragging in the grass, her arms thrown skyward like a Greek goddess summoning the elements. My father had tossed his jacket and his bow tie. His hands were clasped, and I did not need to read lips to know that he was begging her, imploring her to *cálmate, querida*, just please calm down.

My father once told me that although my mother was thin, at heart she was an opera singer. "Her gift is delicate, and she protects it the only way she knows how—with layers and layers of drama," he explained.

I watched, still and unmoving, as my mother went

straight for my father's orchids, dropping pot after pot onto the floor. My father screamed when the first one broke, and for a minute, the look of rage was such that I thought, "That's it. This is the time when he loses his cool and he hits her." But he didn't raise his hand to her; he never has and he promises he never will. Instead, he took her in his arms and she collapsed, crying on his shoulder. And that is where I left them, sitting on a mountain of dirt, orchid petals strewn around them like an exploded Hawaiian lei. My mother was crying and my father was holding her, and I knew that this was the end. The evening's performance was over.

My mother's mood swings were just crazy, especially after Sergio went away to school. When she was happy, it was like the warmth of a thousand suns. When she was angry, it was all hellfire, like her fury could burn the whole house down. But the sadness was the worst. When she was depressed, it was like a slow plague that floated through our house. We couldn't see it or touch it or smell it, but we could all eventually feel what she was feeling—the sadness, the weakness, the bewilderment, the helplessness. It was on those days, when we were all piled on the living room sofa watching Princess Diana or whatever heartbreaking video my mother had locked into, that I feared that it would all fall apart—my mother, my parents' marriage, the oh-so-fragile sticks that made up the walls and roof and door of our family home.

My mom often worked late, so a lot of nights it was just me and Papá for dinner. I didn't mind. Dinners with my father were easy. He never bugged me about eating fattening foods, never urged me to wear more makeup or *haga algo con su cabello*, do something with "that hair." When it was just us, a lot of times we ate in the study in front of the TV. We both loved soccer, and our favorite team was FC Barcelona. When we first started watching, my dad explained to me how Madrid's team had deep roots in Spain's fascist past. But the Barcelona team was more than just a bunch of guys who got together to play soccer. They were freedom fighters and idealists; the team symbolized a belief in equality and good sportsmanship. "*Son hombres,*" my father said of the Barça players, "who understand both the art of living and the art of the game." He turned to me then and said, "Like us."

In real life, I was hardly sporty—a little tennis here and there, a lot of swimming in the summer. But I liked watching soccer with my father, I liked the way he equated our family with the Barcelona team. He didn't have to say it in order for me to get that his lessons about the sport were actually lessons about life. So much of how we lived seemed outsized and unreal. I loved the practicality and easy-to-follow nature of sports.

We were watching Barcelona demolish Manchester United and eating a Hawaiian pizza when my mother walked in.

"You're home early, *querida*," he said, giving her a kiss on the cheek.

I got up to hug her. "*Hola, Mami. Qué tal?*" What's up?

She looked over at our pizza that had been smothered with crushed tomatoes, cheese, ham, pineapple, and bacon. "That looks good," she said. "Can I have a slice?"

This was unusual. My mother never ate pizza. I don't mean she ate it once in a while or when we were on vacation. I mean she ate it never.

My father and I glanced at each other as she quickly gobbled down one slice, then another. "*Qué sabroso*," she said. "Where have you been all my life?"

She was wearing a long tank top, yoga pants, and flip-flops. It was a look she would never wear beyond the four walls of our home. "Illusions must be maintained," she always said by way of explanation when she took two hours to get ready just for brunch or Plaza La Rosa, her favorite mall.

My father was drinking a Dos Equis, and my mother said, "Oooh, I'd like one of those."

Another head scratcher. My mother never drank beer. Tequila with a squeeze of lime, yes. A glass of champagne, occasionally. She said it so often, it was almost a mantra— beer makes you fat. Tonight, as she popped open a bottle of brew, there was no such talk. "I only wish your brother, Sergio, was here," she said, smiling wistfully. "But he's not, so we will fill him in later. There's something I want to tell you."

Then it occurred to me—she was sick. Cancer. It was the only explanation. She was home from work early, with a freshly scrubbed face and a hankering for pizza and beer. I started to cry before she could even get the words out. "Please, no," I whispered.

My mother leapt up and wrapped her arms around me. "What is it? Are you pregnant?"

My father sprung up then, and with tears in his eyes, he

said, "Camilla, no. We'll support you, but God knows, this isn't what we wanted for you."

Mami was crying then too, holding me in her arms and rocking me back and forth. "We'll manage," she kept saying. "We'll manage."

It all happened so fast—the crying, the hugging, the despair. What can I say? We're kind of a high-strung family.

In my head, we were still talking about my mother's illness. "How long have you known?" I asked.

"About what? The pregnancy?" she looked confused. "You just told me."

It was my turn to be confused. "I'm not pregnant. I'm talking about the cancer."

"*Ay Dios*, no!" my father moaned. "Who has cancer?"

I nodded toward my mother. "Mami has cancer."

She looked horrified. "I don't have cancer!"

We all took a deep breath then.

"Let's start over," my mother said, taking a seat on the couch. "Sit with me."

I sat next to my father and leaned my head on his shoulder. Whatever it was, it had to be bad. Carolina del Valle was eating pizza, drinking beer, and wearing sweats. That was Armageddon behavior in my house.

"This is going to sound funny," my mother began, "but I've decided to seek treatment for my . . . anxiety. I used to think it was an occupational hazard—to be an actress meant that your heart had no skin, no covering. But I've been talking to Albita and my agent Samantha and Andy . . ."

"Your hair guy?" my father asked, clearly hurt that he hadn't been included in the conversation.

"What other Andrew could I mean?" my mother asked. "He gives very good advice. He never breaks a confidence. He's like a bartender, I swear."

She continued, "For a long time, I've been wanting to go see a therapist. But I've been afraid that because of my . . . notoriety, anyone I saw in Mexico City would sell my secrets for a quick buck. But Samantha found me someone in LA—a Latina woman who has a lot of celebrity clients. I spoke to the therapist on the phone today. And what I'd like to do is go out to LA for a week after this novela wraps. She'll clear her schedule, and I'll meet with her every day. At the end of the week, we'll make a plan for the next steps."

My father looked sad but relieved at the same time. "I'll come with you, *mi amor*," he said.

"I'll come too," I chimed in.

My mother smiled. "You have school."

I shrugged. "I can miss school. No big deal. I want to be with you . . . and I kind of would love a trip to LA."

She shook her head. "No can do, sweetheart. One, your brother would kill me if I took you out of school for no good reason. He still has dreams of you following in his footsteps to Oxford."

I didn't not want to go to Oxford. I was a pretty good student. But I wasn't Sergio smart. He was always laser focused with his education, like his genius was this giant butterfly, flapping around his brain, desperately trying to get out. I didn't see far into the future the way my brother did. I had no big ideas, no dreams or schemes about my grown-up life. I just woke up each day and tried to be as happy as possible. You couldn't exactly put that on a college application.

Mami took my hand and said, "The other reason that you can't come is because this trip is not a vacation. Araceli, the doctor in LA, has already told me that in looking to manage my emotions, we will probably dredge some tough stuff up. I may feel worse before I feel better."

Having seen Mami at her worst, I understood and didn't press it any further.

"Well, I, for one, feel better already," Papa said, wrapping my mother in a tight embrace. "I'm very proud of you for taking this step, *cariña.*"

"I'm proud of myself," she said, kissing him on the lips.

"Oh, come on! Get a room!" I called out, tossing a throw pillow at them.

My mother laughed, her just-for-us, not-for-TV laugh, and said, "Okay, it's Friday and the night is young. What should we do?"

"Let's watch a movie," my father said.

I jumped up and bolted for the drawers of DVDs in the armoire. *"Entre Amantes!"* I said, holding up the case with the bodice-ripper cover.

My mother groaned. "That old thing!"

"Okay," I said, putting it back. "You're home early. We love you. So you choose."

My mother walked to the cabinet and searched, for what seemed like forever.

"This one," she said, holding up a DVD.

"*Women on the Verge of a Nervous Breakdown?*" I asked. "That movie is a gazillion years old. Isn't it black-and-white?"

"It's not that old," my mother protested. "It's in color."

My father smiled and asked me, "You've never seen it, right?"

"Never."

"Trust me," my mother said, and smiled. "It's perfect."

And it was.

4

★

HEARTBREAKER

One afternoon, after my mother's trip to LA, Patrizia came over after school and said, "Your mom seems like she's in a good mood."

I explained that my mother was doing great. "Her meetings went really well."

"Do you think your mother ever slept with someone to get a part?"

"What?"

"Happens all the time in that industry. Pay to Play, my Dad calls it. But, seriously, she's good? No breaking glass? No diva tantrums?"

I muttered, "Come on, Patti. Stop it." I regretted telling her about my mother, anything personal about our family.

When she came back from the bathroom, she held up a bottle of pills.

"I'm sure these happy pills help, right? Want one?"

"What?" I jumped up, trying to wrest the bottle away from her. "Give those back."

She popped open the bottle, took out two pills, and washed them down with a swig of Coke Zero.

I knew that my mother's therapist had prescribed some pills for her. I didn't know what. It hadn't even occurred to me to search her bathroom and look.

I put the pills back and thought about what Sergio would say if he was around. But I didn't have to imagine. I only had to remember what he'd told me at Christmas: "You're better than that, Cammi. *Mejor sola que mal acompañada.* It's better to be alone than in bad company. You have to know how to cut that kind of person out of your life."

I had managed to forget about the whole situation with Patti and Mami's pills, until I came home from school one day and it was like someone had died. Usually when I walked into the house, there were ten people: Albita and her team in the kitchen, Diana making kale soup for my mother, and the security guys watching soccer on TV in the study. The show's wardrobe designers sometimes came by for fittings, so it wasn't unusual to see them or Marta, my mother's personal shopper, in my mother's dressing room with shopping bags full of clothes for my mother to try on.

But today there was no one cooking in the kitchen.

There was no music playing, no soccer game on the TV. My father and mother sat in the formal dining room, the one we used only for holidays and big dinner parties. Also seated at the long, hand-carved wood table were people I recognized but rarely saw. Samantha Gonzalez, my mother's agent. Javi Cortes, my mom's PR rep.

"What's going on?" I asked.

My father handed me a stack of tabloid newspapers.

My heart sank when I saw the first paper—a big picture of a medicine bottle with my mother's name on it. Prescription: diazepam for anxiety.

My mother looked weak. "Of course, all this press is making me a little anxious."

The headlines just got worse and worse:

CAROLINA DEL VALLE,
THE NOT-SO-HAPPY HOUSEWIFE

THE SWEETHEART OF TEXCOCO
IS MEX-CUKOO, CUCKOO!

CAROLINA DISTRAUGHT AND ON DRUGS, SAYS,
"IVAN SANCOCHO IS MY ONE TRUE LOVE."

My mother was crying, and my father looked like he wanted to hurt someone. Albita was making cups of coffee, which I noticed she was spiking with heavy cream and whiskey.

Javi said, "Let me put this all into perspective. Is it hurtful? Yes. Do you feel vulnerable and exposed? Yes. Am I the least bit concerned? No."

"Me neither," Samantha chimed in. Then she mimed to Albita that she'd like more whiskey in her coffee.

Javi stood in front of my parents as if he were making a presentation at a sales conference. "People are talking about you more than they have in ages, Carolina. There is no such thing as bad press, darling."

"Exactly!" Samantha said. "We will get in front of this, and we will control the story."

Javi snapped his fingers. "Maybe we can use this to get you a spokesperson deal for a pharmaceutical company."

Samantha nodded enthusiastically. "That's not a bad idea."

My mother and father looked up and said, almost in unison, "No."

Samantha jumped sides more quickly than you could say "flip-flop." "It's a terrible idea. No spokesperson deals at this time."

My mother held up all the supermarket rags with photos of her and Ivan Sancocho kissing. Old photos from telenovelas she had filmed before I was born.

"What I hate is how this is bringing all of those old rumors back," she said.

"That's all they are. Rumors," my father murmured lovingly.

I knew then that there was something I needed to do. Find Patrizia. Confront her for selling secrets about my mother. And possibly kill her.

The next morning, I called Patrizia. Before I could say a

word, she said, "Hey, I'm sorry about all the bad press about your mom," her voice dripping with fake sincerity.

"Really, Patti," I said, trying not to sound as angry as I felt.

My father said that whenever he was doing a voice-over for a character who was very powerful, he sat very still. "Powerful people don't fidget," he said. "Fidgeting, nerves, a lack of confidence. You don't need to see a person to know they're losing it. You can hear it in their voice."

I took a deep breath and said, "I really need to talk to you. Can you meet me? Today?"

"Sure thing, C," she said. "I'll be right over."

"No," I told her. "I'll come to you."

My mother was taking a few days off work. The network didn't mind because the TexCoco studio was a zoo. Reporters and photographers swarmed the place. They came from, literally, all over the world—not just Mexico but Miami and all over Latin America, Spain, and Portugal. There were even stringers for the gossip rags in Moscow and eastern Europe, where telenovelas were huge and my mother was a big star.

After I got off the phone with Patrizia, I found Mami sitting in the study, playing cards with my father.

"Not on your iPad?" I asked. Normally my mother was glued to the thing, a dozen windows open with fashion and beauty sites and all her favorite online shopping.

She smiled. "Too tempting to Google myself. I'm cutting myself off for a few days."

I kissed her forehead and said, "It'll be okay, Mami."

"Of course it will," she answered. "It's just, right now things suck. But you know what they say: *la vida es dura pero yo soy más dura.*"

Life is tough, but I am tougher.

"Where are you off to?" my father asked. I could tell he had a good hand because of the little smirk on his face. My father could disguise his voice a hundred ways, but he had no game when it came to poker.

"I'm going to the mall to meet a friend. Is that okay?"

My mother nodded. "Yes. At least one of us should get back to the business of normal life."

"Have Samir drive you," my father said. "And turn around immediately if you start getting followed by the paparazzi."

As the gates to our home opened, reporters and photographers stormed the car.

"It's not her," Samir said, rolling down the window to give them a peek. Assured that their scoop was not driving away, the press returned to their posts.

I had forgotten how frantic it could get, how hunted my mother could feel. I'd spent most of my life thinking she was a narcissist, a good mom but a self-involved diva all the same. I thought about what a huge production my mother's workplace was. Even without the scandal, it must make a person feel happy yet anxious to arrive at work and see giant billboards of herself everywhere she looks. It took so many people to make a telenovela. There were writers, producers, and network executives; set designers, decorators, and construction crews; craft services, trailer managers, location scouts, camera operators, and sound and light techs; not to mention hair, makeup, and wardrobe. Everyone had an assistant, and some of the assistants had assistants, called second assistants. My mom was at the center of it all. Some of the people liked and admired her, but lots of them didn't like her at all, especially other actors who saw her as the one to beat. Sometimes when I visited her on set, she would look over at a crowd of stand-ins and cast members and whisper to me, "Can you feel it? All the hatred coming off that couch?"

Because she was the star, Mami had to be nice to everybody. God forbid she was tired or in a bad mood or had a legitimate beef with someone. She was always acting, even when the cameras weren't rolling, from the moment she arrived until the moment she stepped into her car and drove away. If she didn't, she'd get labeled as "difficult," other people would use her behavior as an excuse for not doing their jobs well, and in the worst-case scenario, this would happen—bad, bad press.

By the time we arrived at Patrizia's house and her security had let us into the compound, I was so mad, I could barely speak. I told Samir that I wouldn't be long.

I walked slowly to the front door, taking deep breaths and trying to stop my heart from racing. I clenched and unclenched my fists, trying to stop my hands from shaking. I reached for the doorbell, but before I could even press it, Patrizia opened the front door.

"Hey, come on in, tell me all about it. *Escándalo!*" she said, grinning.

"I'm not coming in," I said. "I'm here to ask you a simple

question. Did you sell that picture of my mother's prescription bottle to the tabloids?"

Patrizia, like my father, was a terrible poker player. I could see it in her face. She actually looked proud of herself. Still she insisted, "No. Why would I do that? You're my best friend."

I tried to stay very still. I stood up straight and tried not to slouch like the wreck I felt inside. "Few words, Camilla," I told myself silently. "Use few words."

"I don't believe you, Patrizia, and I don't want to be friends with you anymore."

Then I turned around and started walking away. I didn't expect her to start crying, but that's what she did. "Don't do this, Cammi," she sobbed. "I'm so sorry. I'll make it up to you. There's so much going on. I think my parents are getting a divorce. You know how I am. I was just acting out."

I didn't say anything. I just kept walking.

"You're not going to say anything?" Patrizia screamed. "I thought we were friends. But I guess you're just a crazy bitch like your mother."

I stopped and turned to look at her, desperate to say something that would end things, to say the right thing that would crush her to pieces. But there was no point in trying to have the last word. It was over, and I needed to go home and come clean to my parents.

In the car, I got a text from Patrizia. The message read:

> I bet you'll think twice before stealing a man from me again. Amadeo was mine.

I couldn't believe it. She had destroyed my mother's reputation, invaded her privacy, and broken my trust over Amadeo. I knew it wasn't really about him. What she liked was being the alpha in our friendship. She was prettier, richer, more legit, with her businessman father and her country club mom. But when I met Amadeo, when I started needing her less, she didn't like it. As many times as I'd watched *Mean Girls*, I'd never thought it would play out that way in my life.

When I got home, I handed the phone to Albita. "Could you block this number, please?"

She looked down at the number and hissed, "I knew it was her."

My parents were sitting in the kitchen. I told them what Patrizia had done and how I had confronted her. "I'm so sorry," I said. Now I was the one in tears.

My father, ever the wise Yoda, said, "We can't control what other people do. You can only control your reaction to them."

For the most part, throughout her career, my mother has gotten along with her costars. There was just one, rather notorious, exception—a high-maintenance tantrum thrower from the Dominican Republic called Ivan Sancocho. The studio had him under contract early in my mother's career, so they begged her to do just one novela, *Entre Amantes*, with him and then she could go back to working with her favorite costars.

From the beginning of the production, my mother and Ivan were at each other's throats. According to Sergio, my mother insisted that his breath smelled. She refused to kiss him unless he brushed his teeth, in front of her, before every love scene. A production assistant brought Ivan a toothbrush, toothpaste, a bucket, and a bottle of water for him to do the deed while my mother watched. "It was humiliating," Sergio told me. "So Ivan began planning his revenge."

Ivan bribed the script supervisor so that my mother didn't get the right draft of the script. She showed up on set after a long weekend, having memorized the wrong lines. If you know my mother, you know that the anxiety of having memorized the wrong lines would drive her crazy. Then he arranged for the studio valets who washed my mother's car every week to call her, distraught, claiming that the car had been stolen. Then, as the final straw, he had the seamstress on the show take in all of my mother's costumes so it would appear that she was gaining weight. Furious, my mother went and complained to the head of the studio. My mother was the telenovela golden girl. Fans loved her, the media was smitten with her, and, most important, advertisers adored her. So the studio agreed—after *Entre Amantes*, Ivan Sancocho would be Ivan San Adios.

The fans had a different idea, however. They made *Entre Amantes* the highest-rated telenovela of the decade. Ivan Sancocho was Ivan Going Nowhere. Adding to the drama, it turned out that Ivan hadn't arranged to have my mother's costumes altered. By the time *Entre Amantes* wrapped, she was three months pregnant with Sergio. By the time the series aired, my mother was eight months pregnant and showing big-time. After Sergio was born, rumors began to fly that

Ivan was actually Sergio's father, and my mother had her first breakdown—a mix of postpartum depression and *Ay, yo no puedo.* I just can't take it.

When I got back from confronting Patrizia, there was a giant bouquet of flowers on the kitchen island. It was crazy big, like one of those standing arrangements you see at a fancy restaurant or at a funeral. "What's this?" I asked.

My mother said, "You want a laugh? Look at the card."

I got up and opened it. It was from Ivan Sancocho. He had written:

> *My darling Carolina,*
> *I have read with sadness about your*
> *recent tragedies. I know you miss me and*
> *that your career has been on a slow nosedive*
> *since our legendary pairing. I can only pray*
> *that one day, before this life is over, your*
> *heart will mend and you find the peace and*
> *happiness that you deserve.*
> *Yours and always yours,*
> *Ivan*

"Are you kidding me?" I said. "What a dick!"

My mother smiled and tipped an imaginary hat at me. "My thoughts exactly."

Then we laughed, all of us, for the first time since the tabloid clouds had opened and hailed down upon our home. I knew that it wasn't going to be easy, and it was actually my fault, but it was going to be okay.

5

★

NO MORE NOVELAS

"Look at this," my mother said, slamming a script down onto the kitchen table. Then, before my father could reach for it, she scooped it back up.

"I won't do it," she insisted, pacing around the kitchen. "I won't pimp the details of my real life and my real struggles for ratings. Those cowardly executives sent me the script on a Saturday because they did not want me to barge into their offices and tell them off. They think I'll cool down by Monday. Well, they're wrong about that." Then she let off a string of curses that was so vitriolic that both my father and I jumped as if the words might hit one of us on their way out the door.

She slammed the script down again. "Reinaldo, you read it. Tell me what you think."

Then my mother turned to me and said, "I can't eat breakfast. Come with me for a swim?" I said yes.

I went upstairs to my bedroom and changed into a simple one-piece. When I got to the pool, my mother was already in the water. She was wearing a two-piece, and even though she had twenty-plus years on me, she had the kind of abs that would make the girls at my school jealous. "Pilates," is what she always said whenever anyone complimented her figure. But I knew the truth: it took a lot more than Pilates to keep my mom looking like a real-life Wonder Woman. She ran on the treadmill every morning for at least forty-five minutes to an hour. If her call time was seven a.m., she was up at five to bang out an hour of cardio in our home gym. Diana, the chef, kept a careful count of every calorie that went into my mother's mouth. If she went out to lunch, for example, she not only ordered sensibly, but she also took a snap with her iPhone of what she ate so that Diana could plan dinner accordingly. Yes, four days a week, she did Pilates with Simone, the French ballerina, who came to the house to put my mother through her paces on the Reformer. But she also lifted weights with Raul, her driver, at least two days a week—light weights, a lot of reps, so that she didn't bulk up. And at least twice a week, either during her lunch break or after work, she went to a spin class. On Saturdays, she ran five to seven miles on the treadmill. And on Sundays, she rested, and by "rest," I mean she went to a spa where she lay under infrared lights for an hour to sweat out all the toxins. This was followed by a sixty-minute lymphatic massage. Each session allegedly burned two thousand calories and offered a "thirty-six-hour metabolic boost."

Watching my mother in the pool, the thought occurred to me that I had no idea how to be a woman, a regular woman. The girls at my school always said I was lucky to have such an amazing woman for my mother, and I was. I loved her. I admired her. But I never labored under the delusion that I could ever be like her. My mother was a goddess. I was a mere mortal.

We swam together in the pool in relative silence. I was lost in my thoughts, and my mother, I knew, was swept away by all the ways that her carefully constructed life was being challenged. When I was very little and I swam in the pool with my mother, I used to pretend that I was a girl from the mainland and that my mother was a mermaid. I pretended that if I followed her, closely and quietly, she would lead me to Atlantis, that lost kingdom under the sea. I thought of that again, as my mother led in laps. I stayed in my own lane, careful not to splash her, intent on not turning until she had made each turn.

After about an hour, my father came out and sat on a chair by the edge of the pool.

"I've read it," he said.

My mother hoisted herself up onto the ledge so she was sitting with her legs dangling in the pool. I did the same.

"So, what do you think?" she asked.

"I don't think you should do it," he answered.

She hugged him then, even though she was soaking wet and he was dressed for golf.

The script the studio had sent my mother was about a high-flying corporate executive, the lone woman in a man's world. She's struggling to keep up, and her boss tells her that she either raises her numbers in the next quarter or she can find another job. Desperate and exhausted, she's sure that she's sunk. Then one day, she accidentally takes her son's ADHD medicine, mistaking it for ibuprofen. On the medicine, she has more energy than she's had in months, she's laser-focused, and she seals a big deal. Thus begins a cycle of pill popping and prescription medicine abuse that ends in shame, destruction, and eventually redemption.

"I'm on antidepressants," my mother said quietly. "I do not have an addiction. My biggest fear about this script is that women who need help—who know a little of my story and watch a lot of telenovelas—won't get the help they need because it seems like I went down a bad road. Asking for help was the best thing I ever did. I don't want to pretend that it's not."

We sat in silence for a while. The sun was hot and it felt good to have my legs in the pool. I knew then that I was wrong when I looked at the externals and thought because I was not va-va-voom like my mother, she was not teaching me something about life.

"Take some time off. Let's call it a sabbatical," my father said decisively. "You've been doing these novelas back-to-back for twenty years. You deserve a vacation. A paid vacation."

We took short holidays—a week here and there, two

weeks at Christmastime. But my father was right. My mother was always, always working.

She looked around nervously. "Reinaldo, maybe that's going too far. You know how fickle this industry can be. It's so hard to stay on top. There's always someone looking to take your place."

My father—sweet, wise, and warm—said firmly, "It's only the top if it's the top you've chosen. If you let the business dictate your value and your worth, then you'll always lose, no matter how many billboards they put your picture on. Tell your agent that you are politely declining this script and you want to spend some time with your family. Tell her to make it clear to the studio that you've earned a six-month paid sabbatical, or you will use the exit clause in your contract. Let them film their *basura* script, and then in six months, when it's in the can, you'll be back."

Mami took a breath and smiled. I could tell she liked the plan. "Even if they say yes—which they won't, but it doesn't hurt to ask—I mean, what would I do with all that time?"

"Maybe we can travel," my father said. "Spend some time in Europe, be a little closer to Sergio."

My father had said the magic word—"Sergio."

"I love that idea," my mother said.

"Hey," I said. "What about me?"

My father took a moment to consider the possibilities. "It's November," he said. "If we take you out of school for the next semester, we could try to get you into a school abroad or maybe get you a tutor. Would you mind?"

I thought about Patrizia. We didn't go to the same school. But in a short time, she'd become my most valued friend, until she wasn't. The other girls at my school were nice—Yvette, Luchina, Denise—girls to hang out with at lunchtime and after school, but no one I'd miss if my family went away for a few months. And how cool it would be to spend a semester in Europe and be closer to Sergio. I was in.

The plan began to take shape, and we began to slowly arrange all the pieces. My mother turned down the script, *Sin Límites*. The studio—maybe out of guilt, maybe out of loyalty—agreed to the sabbatical. My mother feared that allowing the sabbatical meant they were grooming someone new, but my father explained that such fears came with the territory. "You are spreading your wings, my love," he said. "It's only natural to wonder if they will hold you up."

Samantha, my mother's agent, found us a fabulous apartment in Madrid. Sergio would only be a two-hour flight away instead of the current ten-hour haul. When Sergio told my mother that he was clearing his schedule and he'd come to see us every weekend, my mother wept. Happy tears. Not Princess Diana tears.

It was now two weeks before Christmas, and we were all set to go to Europe right after New Year's when Samantha came by the house to talk to my mother. She said, "You know how they say that when you make plans, God laughs?"

It turned out that while my mother had been in LA having her head shrunk, she'd squeezed in a few "getting to know you" meetings with producers. One of the producers had been so taken with my mother that, unbeknownst to her, he'd kept her in mind for a new series he was developing. It would be for a major network, in English, and he wanted my mother to be one of the stars. If it was successful, it would be one of the biggest breaks in my mother's already considerable career. If it failed, Samantha reasoned, then we would return to Mexico and my mother would go back to work at TexCoco. LA had never been part of the plan. But this last-minute plot twist, so very telenovela, was too juicy to resist. My mother said yes. We all said yes. How could we not?

Suddenly we were heading to LA, and life would change for all of us.

PART TWO

LA/Hollywood

6

★

JET SET

We'd visited the United States before. Ever since I was little, my mother had been traveling to Miami to do press for her shows. A press junket is when a studio is promoting a project. They fly a bunch of reporters to a hotel and ensconce my mother in a giant suite, and she gives interviews from eight a.m. to eight p.m. When we were younger, Sergio and I would travel with her and we loved it. Fancy hotels. Room service. Hanging out by the pool. And the big bonus: everybody in Miami spoke Spanish, or at least so it seemed. My father would urge us to practice our English, insisting that the younger you are when you learn, the less of an accent you have. So we became fluent in Spanglish — switching back and forth between English and Spanish.

But my mother hated the press junkets. "They always ask the same questions," she'd complain. "What are your favorite designers? What do you do in your free time? What's your biggest dream? What's your greatest fear?" She would roll her eyes and say, "How many different ways can I say it? Chanel and Gucci, depends on the occasion. I have no free time because when my show isn't shooting, I'm holed up in a hotel room with the likes of you. My biggest dream is for you to go away. My biggest fear is that you'll never leave and I'll be stuck in this hotel room answering inane questions until I die, preternaturally young, from boredom."

I've mentioned that she's dramatic, right? But the funny thing is that because she speaks so quickly, what might sound like a speech in English comes off as more like a side comment in Spanish. Speedy Gonzales isn't really a stereotype; his speech pattern is totally accurate.

Sometimes we went to Miami for red carpet events, like the Latin Music Awards. My mother liked these a lot more. I never got to go with her to an event—my father was always her date—but really the party started way before she hit the red carpet. Watching my mother get ready for a big awards show was like watching the Fairy Godmother transform Cinderella for the ball. The studio would rent a whole apartment-sized suite for my mother's team of stylists to come with what my mother called *los contendientes,* the contenders—a dozen or more dresses that my mother had chosen from runway photos but that she hadn't actually tried on.

Each dress had pinned to its garment bag a photo with

a corresponding hairstyle: an elaborate updo for a strapless dress with an Old Hollywood feel, a faux bob for a more modern dress with a dramatic asymmetrical hemline, loose beachy waves to soften a tuxedo-style dress. Two giant Louis Vuitton trunks held all her *lenceria*—the shapewear, bras, and undies that were the perfect undergarments for whatever dress she chose.

Once my mother had picked her dress (and I'd tried on one or two of the ones she'd rejected), we ordered lunch: burgers for me and my dad, salads for the stylists and glam squad, and one large green juice (sometimes a beet juice with greens) for my mom. She couldn't risk eating and being bloated on the big day. Then after lunch, the jewelry guys arrived, men in dark suits with earphones subtly tucked into their shirt collars. They looked like a presidential detail, the Secret Service or FBI agents, but their black leather suitcases gave them away. They were carrying hundreds of thousands of dollars' worth of diamonds. #Blingbaby.

That was the extent of my American experience. We never went to schools or even malls. When we went to restaurants, we were whisked from our SUV to private dining rooms. Which is all to say that as our plane touched down at Santa Monica airport, it occurred to me that as many times as I had visited the US, it was always under the steam of my mother's work. I did not have and had never made an American friend. I did not know American girls my own age except for the ones I had watched on TV dramas about boarding schools and about girls in small towns who might or might not be guilty of murder. That being said, I knew, maybe more than most, just how much you shouldn't believe everything you saw on TV.

We flew private to LA, a tiny jet with just eight seats in two mini seating areas, one at the front of the plane and one at the back. The inside of the plane had beautiful, honey-colored leather seats. As we threw our bags into the chairs opposite us, my father and I both took a whiff and said, "*Aroma de carro nuevo,*" new car smell. Then we looked at each other and said, "*Encantado! Me debes un refresco!*"

"Jinx, you owe me a Coke" isn't really something you say in Mexico, but my dad had learned it in one of his voice-over roles and he, Sergio, and I have been saying it ever since I was a kid.

My mother wasn't exactly afraid of flying, but she was superstitious. She always sat in the back of the plane, listening to Spanish covers of the Beatles' "Blackbird." Only when she'd heard the song three times through would she come and join me and my father.

When she finished listening to her song, she came over and squeezed my hand. "This is so exciting! We're going to Hollywood."

"You're going to Hollywood," I corrected her. "I'm going to a new school."

She didn't look worried. "But you love school!"

Not true. "Sergio looooves school. I like school okay."

"Like is good," my mother said, in Spanish, as the flight attendant handed her a Coke Zero. My father had suggested that when we arrived in California, we speak English at home. But we weren't there yet.

"I couldn't stand school," my mother continued. "I was a bad student."

This was something I knew. "But you were beautiful and talented, so you became a rich and famous actress."

"I wasn't so beautiful," my mother insisted. "And nobody thought I was that talented. In fact, I was pretty average. . . ."

Como yo. I urged her to complete the sentence. She was pretty average, like me.

It's not that it wasn't true. I knew that I was average. I didn't want her to lie to me. But not wanting to be lied to isn't exactly the same thing as wanting to hear the truth.

My father, sensing a tense moment, jumped in. "So how's that fellow of yours?"

I smiled. "He's good."

When I found out we were moving to LA, I made Amadeo promise that we could take a break. Not for my sake, for his. He was a college guy dating a high school girl. I couldn't help but think that once he fell for someone his own age, that would be it. And I honestly thought that hearing about him falling in love with another girl would be easier if I was twenty-five hundred miles away.

We were hanging out at my favorite little caf in Coyoácan when I first broached the topic. "You want to date American guys," he said.

"It's not that," I told him. "You should see other girls. I mean, women. You're practically old enough to get married."

He guffawed. "Married?"

I smiled. "My mother got married when she was twenty."

"So did mine. But that was a different generation."

I was insistent. "I still think we should take a break."

He leaned in to kiss me. Then when I reached for him, he pulled away.

"None of that," he said flirtatiously. "We're on a break."

I scowled. "The break will obviously start after I leave for California."

Then he kissed me and said, "You're going to miss me."

"Of course I will," I answered. "But we can video chat."

He said no. "If we're going on a break, then no calls, no chats. It's going to be easy for you. You're going to be in LA, hanging out with movie stars and meeting all those cool American guys. Six months is going to feel like a vacation for you. I'll be in school, practicing procedures on cadavers. I'll be lucky if anyone even wants to have coffee with me, as I'll smell of formaldehyde."

I laughed.

"*Voy a ser infeliz,*" he said. I'm going to be miserable.

He said it with so much feeling that I actually believed him.

Amadeo and I said goodbye so many times in the days leading up to our move. Each time, I promised that I would not call him or text once I got to LA. But the plane was in the air and we hadn't landed yet. So I figured I was legitimately, and cloud-wise, in the gray zone.

I went to the back of the plane and hit the video chat screen. When he appeared, he looked more sad than bothered.

"Cammi, you promised."

"But we haven't landed in LA yet," I said cheerfully. "Miss me?"

He sighed. "*Sí. Claro que sí.*"

"I'm glad."

"I have a great idea," he said. "Let's not break up."

"We are not breaking up!" I told him. "We're taking *un pequeño* break."

We talked for a few minutes. I kissed the phone again and again. Then we said goodbye, the way we always did.

"You're crazy," he said.

"And you like it," I answered, hitting the End Call button.

7

★

90210

Four hours. That's all it takes to fly from Mexico City to LA. Less than the time it takes to fly from New York to California. But when you're coming from south of the border, everything is different.

When we arrived at the Santa Monica airport, an immigration official met our plane and escorted us to a plush lounge. A few minutes later, he returned with our passports and my parents' work visas. A town car was waiting for us and we were off to the Chateau Marmont, which would be our home away from home until we got settled. We had officially come to the USA. We weren't exactly Mexican immigrants.

At the hotel, my mother was registered under her real

name: Carolina del Valle. No cheeky pseudonym, borrowing the names of Mexican silent-movie stars, like the ones she liked to use when we checked into hotels—Fanny Aritua or Oralia Dominguez.

My mother's new show was what they call a backdoor pilot. The character would be introduced through a few cameo appearances on an existing hit show. Then in the summer, when that show went on hiatus, my mother's show would be introduced.

The show that my mother would appear on first was called *Shot Callers.* It was a one-hour drama about four Harvard biz school grads who are all married and living in the suburbs as stay-at-homes. None of the women are using their degrees, and they're not happy about it. When one of the women's fathers leaves her a sizable inheritance, they decide to band together and start an online retail business. The business is called Lady Parts, and every month it sends each subscriber a box full of her favorite drugstore items, from tampons to deodorants. The business is a huge success, and that's where the drama starts.

The spin-off series begins when Kelly James, one of the main characters on *Shot Callers,* is cut out of the Lady Parts business. Determined to prove her frenemies wrong, she buys a homemade hot sauce recipe from her maid, María José, played by my mother. The ten-thousand-dollar fee is enough for María José to buy a house—cosigned by Kelly. But it's not enough for her to quit her job. The new show, called *Scoville Units,* follows the two characters as the success of Kelly's Kaboom Sauce forces the women to renegotiate their relationship from employer and domestic to business partners.

"You see," my mother said. "It's not like I'm *really* a maid. I'm a woman with ambition. Like Melanie Griffith in *Working Girl* or Jennifer Lawrence in *Joy.*"

It didn't bother me. I didn't see any stigma attached to my mother playing a maid. It was just another part, right?

Bright and early the morning after we landed, our real estate agent arrived to show us houses. My parents were hopeful about my mother's TV role and decided to rent a place for the year to come.

We took the elevator to the lobby, and I heard the agent before I saw her. "María Carolina Josefina del Valle y Calderón!" she screamed, using my mother's full birth name in true superfan fashion. "It's you! You're even more beautiful in person."

The real estate agent was a thirtysomething Latina with dark blond hair, rocking hot-pink lipstick and a bright turquoise sheath dress. Basically, she was like the poster child for my mother's fans.

My mother looked so pleased that I was worried that the agent could've shown her a one-room shack with a dirt floor and an outhouse and my mother would have said, "*Mundial!* We'll take it!"

The agent's name was Digna Durán, and when she led us to her car, a black Range Rover, it was my dad's turn to smile.

"I love this car. I have one in Mexico. May I drive?" he asked.

Digna smiled and said, "Sure, why not. I heard your takeover of the *Rev Arriba* podcast. You know a lot more about cars."

As I got into the backseat, I have to say, I was impressed. A lot of people knew about my mother. But to be able to quote an obscure car-fan national radio podcast that my dad hosted every once in a while? Digna Durán was *good.* In the car, Digna told us she was born in Costa Rica but grew up in Los Angeles.

My parents were seated in the front, and Digna was in the back with me. She turned to me and said quietly, not so loud that my parents could hear her, "You are so lucky to have Carolina del Valle as your mother." I tried not to fake wretch. In case I was missing life in Mexico City, here it was, back in my face: "You've got a famous mom; you're a spoiled little MAP" (Mexican American Princess).

Then Digna said, "You're so pretty. You're like a taller version of her."

This was not true. But I appreciated the compliment, especially the way that Digna spoke directly and quietly to me. She wasn't doing what most people did, which was say nice things about me in front of my mother, in an attempt to get on my mother's good side.

I'd been to LA on short trips before. When I was very little, my parents took me and Lydia Sepúlveda, my best friend from the second grade, to Disneyland. Then a few times, in the years since, we all came up for a weekend when my mother had an event to attend. Most of the Latin media was in Miami, so we went there far more often.

I texted Sergio:

> I heart LA. It's like a country club compared to Mexico City.

He wrote back:

> Mexico City so dense bc they stole California from us. Remember?

I smiled. You could count on my brainiac bro to bring up the subject of historical misappropriation. I texted back:

> I thought Switzerland was neutral?

He wrote:

> Mexican heart. Clocking francs. Money over everything, sis.

I laughed. Whenever one of us wanted to end a conversation on a light note, we quoted a line from one of our favorite comedy albums by Hannibal Buress: "Money over everything." Long story. Well, short story. But the point is, it always made us laugh.

Digna showed us houses all over town. The valley was

a short drive to the studio, but it was too far from the beach for my mother. "I finally get to live in LA," she said. "I want to be close to the beach."

My father and I fell in love with a beautiful three-story modern house in Venice. It had views of the ocean and a roof deck, and it was literally a ten-minute walk to the beach. I snapped a selfie in front of the house and texted it to my brother. He texted me back a thumbs-up.

After a thorough tour, my mother shook her head. "It's pretty, but I don't like it," she said. "It's a box upon a box on top of a box. It's got coffin energy."

We were standing on the roof of the house, and the California sun was so bright, it was like something out of a music video. Digna, however, seemed to hear my mother's concern. "Point taken," she said. "Please keep in mind, I know an *excellent* feng shui guy. All my celeb clients love him."

My mother looked intrigued but not appeased. As we stood on the roof, staring out at the Pacific Ocean, she turned to us and said, "I want to look at houses in Beverly Hills."

Digna said, "Give me ten minutes. I'll pull together a few listings."

My mother sat down in a lounge chair. My father sat to one side of her, and I sat on the other. She said, "You know, when I was your age, maybe a little younger, there used to be a TV show called *Beverly Hills, 90210*. It was all about teenagers in Beverly Hills. I never thought back then that I could live in a place like that."

Which is how we ended up in a 1920s Spanish colonial

in Beverly Hills. After my parents signed the lease, I texted
another selfie to Sergio and wrote:

Home Sweet Home.

He sent me a series of emojis back:

I wrote him back:

Exactly.

8

★

THE DOMESTIC

The next day, my mother invited me to come along to the studio for her first costume fitting. When we arrived at the Skift Studios, I could see it was a lot like TexCoco. Heavy-duty security to even get on the lot—check. Big airport hangar-style buildings for all of those sets—check. Sets that looked like life-sized dollhouses—two walls and a living room here, three walls and a kitchen there? Yes. Air-conditioning on turbo so everyone was freezing? Check, check, checkity, check.

We were met outside Stage 16 by my mother's new American agent, Lucy Cortés. Lucy was from Colombia, petite and pretty, with an "It's handled" authority. We all kissed hello, Latin style. Then she said, "None of the leads for the show is shooting today, so we'll just go in for a quick tour and then over to wardrobe. We'll introduce you to the cast and the crew more formally next week."

Even though they weren't shooting, the stage was abuzz with action: carpenters were building sets, lighting engineers were testing cues, set decorators were running back and forth to the storage rooms. In Mexico, it would have been "all hail the one and only Carolina del Valle," but this was different. No one recognized my mother. For all they knew, we were nobodies, the country cousins of a production assistant, or sweepstakes winners cashing in on a tour.

"It's kind of nice to fly under the radar," my mother whispered to me, because, of course, she noticed it too.

I agreed, but I was embarrassed that the word "nobodies" had even flashed through my mind. My parents hadn't raised me that way. "This elite status we enjoy is a fabrication of a culture that makes the little people you see on your TV screens into BFDs—big f***ing deals," my father liked to say. He said the real BFDs are the heroes of real life—the teachers, the doctors, the firefighters; the people who walk toward danger, not away from it; the dreamers who were committed to changing the world. I was none of those things. Just a girl who was lucky enough that my mother's job meant that I'd never wanted for anything in my life.

We took a golf cart over to wardrobe. I'm not a big fan of golf, but I *love* to ride a golf cart around a television studio. At TexCoco, my mother had her own cart and driver, with her name, Carolina, on the license plate. In wardrobe, Lucy introduced us to the wardrobe heads, Gabrielle and

Margo. There were clothes, tape, pins, and other quick-tailoring tools in neat piles everywhere. I instantly felt at home. I'd been coming with my mother to wardrobe fittings for as long as I could remember. When I was really small, it seemed like my mother trailed sequins everywhere she went. I used to collect all the sequins that fell off her magical, Las Vegas diva–style dresses, and I would make art projects out of them. I glued them to my notebooks and onto the birthday cards and Mother's Day cards that I made for my mother. Later, when I was a little older, Roxanne and Nelly, my mother's wardrobe queens at TexCoco, would help me sew the fallen sequins into outfits for my Barbie dolls.

The wardrobe women are some of the most important people on set because they're the ones who help the star look good. They know what colors and cuts will make you look amazing and how to hide your every figure flaw. My mother says, "Those women have more tricks than Harry Potter's spell book." The thing is that they have to *like* you to make you look fabulous. So the relationship is an important one to maintain. In Mexico City, my mother always made sure to remember Roxanne's and Nelly's birthdays and all of their special occasions, and she never skimped on the presents. Diamonds and other valuables were not out of the question.

So it was a good sign when Gabrielle said, "Oh my God, that body! You're going to be a joy to dress."

My mother beamed. "Pilates."

But then they handed my mother a dove-gray French

maid uniform with white cuff sleeves and a little white apron. I could tell that she was dying a little bit inside.

"Is this it?"

"Yeah, hon," Margo said. "Your character is a maid."

My mother smiled tightly. "But she's not a maid twenty-four hours a day. Doesn't she have any off-duty clothes? Maybe she goes out dancing on a Saturday night with her friends?"

Gabrielle and Margo exchanged a glance.

My mother had never had a one-outfit part in her entire life, and I honestly thought she might burst into tears on the spot. "She's Latin. She's Catholic," my mother said. "Doesn't she go to church on Sunday? Certainly she won't be wearing *that* to church."

Gabrielle sighed and said, "The producers didn't ask us to pull any other clothes. But maybe we got our wires crossed."

Lucy, my mother's new agent, jumped into the fray. "Well, this is just the start. As your character develops from domestic to entrepreneur to mogul, I promise you the fabulous is coming."

My mother just nodded.

"First thing next week, we'll set up meetings for you with all of the major stylists in town," Lucy continued. "We'll let them know that their marching orders are to find you the coolest, most elegant, most edgy outfits for all of the network events."

My mother, characteristically boisterous and overly

friendly, just whispered, "Okay, thanks." Then she took the maid's uniform and stepped into the curtained changing room.

When she came out, it was a clear contradiction—my mother in full makeup and perfect hair blow-out in this dowdy uniform.

Margo cleared her throat as if summoning her courage, and said, "I totally don't want to mess up your beautiful hair, but I think the producers would like to see your hair back."

She handed my mother a bright orange hair tie, and my mother took it from her like it was something that had been dropped in the toilet.

"Thanks," my mother said quietly.

I looked at her and tried to imagine her in this other life. Usually my mother's roles didn't mean that much to me. Over the years, in her novelas, she has played a detective, a construction worker, half a dozen heiresses, and at least two black widow female serial killers. But watching her get into character as María José was different. My mother came to the US with a nice fancy immigration lawyer to fix our papers and a studio to help us get sorted with a high-end real estate agent, a bank account, a private school, and all the things that had made coming here easy. What would have happened to us if we'd come here the way so many less fortunate Mexican immigrants did? What would our lives have been like if we'd come illegally? I hadn't considered this before.

Watching my mother in a maid's uniform, pulling her

hair back, I could see her starting to find María José inside herself; the process of becoming that is my mother's job.

When Margo said, "Just a few quick Polaroids," my mother's smile for the camera was one that I had never seen before—a mixture of exhaustion and humility, politeness and just the tiniest spark of possibility. Then she winked at me and whispered, *"Bienvenida a los Estados Unidos."* Welcome to the United States.

9

★

MEXICAN KITCHEN

It was my first day at a progressive school that Lucy, my mother's agent, said was *amazing*. "It's got the academics of Harvard and the social scene of Aspen all rolled into one," she said. "You're going to love it."

My father had wanted me to go to Harvard-Westlake. "It's most like your school at home, academically rigorous, uniforms. . . ."

I fake punched him on the shoulder. "You just like the fact that 'Harvard' is in the name."

He smiled. "What father doesn't want to say his daughter goes to Harvard?"

But from the moment I set foot on the campus of Polestar, I wanted in. I wanted LA to be a fresh start, for everything to be different. I wanted to forget some of who I'd become with Patrizia and see if I could become someone new.

The boy who'd been assigned to show me around reminded me of the brown-haired boy in the English-language books my father used to buy for me when I was very small, *A Leer con Dick y Jane*. Read with Dick and Jane. He had the same sandy-brown hair, a similar blue polo shirt, and short khaki pants. He was dressed in character, and Polestar didn't even require uniforms.

The school was as big as a college campus, and already I was afraid of getting lost. There was a science lab and a library, a theater, a football field, tennis courts, a pool, squash courts, an arts and humanities building, a history and philosophy building. It just went on and on.

My old school was one big building with six floors. It looked like the dark, brick monastery that it once had been. Polestar, in comparison, was like a small city. When we got to the cafeteria, my guide—his name was Ethan—started to point out the tables as if they were habitats in a zoo. "Those are the jocks," he said. "I mostly hang with them, despite the fact that this conservative cauldron won't recognize ultimate Frisbee as a real sport."

He pointed around the room like a second hand making its way around a clock. "Those are the nerds. Those are the druggies. Those are the trustafarians. And over there are your peeps—the Mexicans."

My peeps. The Mexicans.

I took a look at a table of dark-haired kids, all dressed in black. One girl was gorgeous. In Mexico, we would have called her a Goth. Although, as Sergio explained it to me, in the DF (District Federal, which is what people from Mexico call Mexico City), Goth, punk, and electronica all blended together into its own weird mash-up of a scene. But whatever. The girl had shoulder-length black hair, although, on one side, it was shaved. She also had tattoos up and down both arms. She was wearing a black-and-white graffiti-print top, black cargo pants, and smart black leather brogues. It wasn't my style, but she had tons of style.

She caught me staring at her and looked me up and down. I wondered, for a second, if she recognized me or if she had instantly sized me up as a new girl, immigrant from the planet Doesn't Have a Clue.

After the tour, Ethan deposited me at my homeroom class into the charge of a very colorfully dressed young man named James. "Call me James," he said. "Never Jimmy. Or else!" Then he burst out laughing. I didn't really get the joke, but that was happening a lot. My English was good. I'd been speaking it my whole life. But then someone would say something and—whoosh!—it went straight over my head.

James asked me to introduce myself to the class. I stood in front of eighteen sets of bored-looking eyeballs and said, "My name is Camilla del Valle."

"Where are you from, Camilla del Valle?" James made the double *l*s in my name into *y*s, which was correct, but he dragged them out so that they sounded like a yodel—*Camiyyyyyyyyya* del *Vayyyyyyye*.

I smiled and said, "Nice accent, James." Then I turned

to the classroom and said, "I'm from Mexico City and I'm really excited to be living in California."

That afternoon, I had a really strange class. They called it Tapestries, the class where you spilled your soul in an attempt to bond with your classmates. The gym was dark and all of the students sat in a circle around an iron pit with what must have been thirty or forty candles. You could actually feel the warmth of the flames on your face. It reminded me of the last night of camp the summer before, in Santander. The counselors threw a bonfire party on the beach. Patrizia and I wore matching sundresses that we'd bought in town. She hooked up with a soccer player named Rafa, and I spent the night with Ibrahim, just sitting on the beach and talking (and kissing) until the sun came up.

The Tapestries teacher was a tall, skinny guy who looked like he was barely out of college. His name was Thomas Smythson, but he insisted we call him Smitty. It was a strange thing for me, coming from Mexico, to have a teacher insist on being called by his first name or by a nickname.

When all the students had settled into a circle around the blazing candles, Smitty explained how Tapestries worked. The class was modeled after a Native American council. The point was to "find our voices and hone our muscles of respect, compassion, and empathy." The "talking stick" (whoever had it was the only one allowed to speak) was crisscrossed with ribbons of the school's colors, navy and yellow. Smitty explained that when the person with the stick was talking, the rest of us honored them with our silence or by softly calling out "A-ho," which is Native American for "I hear you, brother" or "I hear you, sister."

One of the boys shouted, "Hey, Smitty, are you sure 'A-ho' isn't Native American for 'I hear you're a slut'?"

The look on Smitty's face suggested that he'd heard that stupid joke before and he was not amused. "Not acceptable, Duncan," he said. "Please come see me after council."

He went on to explain that students are graded in Tapestries based on three components: attendance, depth of participation, and emotional growth. It seemed like a complicated metric, and I must have looked concerned, because the girl next to me whispered, "Don't sweat it, blondie. Everyone gets an A."

The first person to share in Tapestries that day was a boy. He took the stick and said, "My name's Simon. My truth is that my father has left my mother for some basic bitch. Nothing earth-shattering there, except we've just found out that my father won't give my mother the house. She can't afford to buy him out, so we're moving to a condo on Barrington, divorce central. Mostly I just feel bad for my mom."

I was surprised. I couldn't imagine a boy at my old school in Mexico City sharing such a personal story with a group of classmates.

Smitty called on a girl named Leigh next, and she took the stick from him shyly. "My name is Leigh," she said softly. "I smoke too much pot. When I get tired of it, I'll stop." Then she sat down.

Wait? What?

I couldn't believe that a student would admit to a teacher, in a public forum, to her drug use. But you would have thought that the Leigh girl was a rapper who'd just spit some crazy cool lyrics, because all of the kids were clapping and stomping their heels like they were at a concert. Smitty tried to put an end to the "woot-woots" by repeating "A-ho! A-ho!" But folks weren't hearing him.

Then he turned to me and said, "Camilla, since you're new, why don't you take the talking stick next?"

Red lights flashed across my brain. Every cell in my body was screaming noooooooooooooo. You don't put the new girl on the spot on her first day. Any Native American elder worth his salt could've told Smitty that. Not cool, bro. Just not cool.

I took the stick and spoke as quickly as I could. "My name's Camilla. I'm from Mexico City. Really looking forward to starting a new life in America."

There were a few tepid calls of "A-ho." That girl Leigh was a tough act to follow.

Then I heard it, softly at first and then louder. That tool, Duncan, was singing something stupid to the tune of that song from *West Side Story*:

I so happy to be in America.
Crawled under barbed wire to
Get to America.
Everything free in America.
Drug cartel no look for me
In America.

Smitty's face looked as red as mine felt. I knew how some people felt about Mexicans. I just didn't think that I'd have to face it on day one. Smitty escorted Duncan to the gym door with strict instructions for him to go directly to the school office. As I watched him go, all I could think was, "Wow. That kid is really stupid."

I don't know why I didn't eat lunch at "the Mexican table." But that day, and for the entire first two weeks, I ate alone. And the food at Polestar was off the hook. Every day, there was something on the menu I'd never tasted before. The school chef, Chef Rooney, had a blog, so I began to read that during my lunch hour.

N'awlins Monday. Where y'all at?

In New Orleans, where I grew up, Monday is for red beans and rice. Traditionally, you throw whatever leftover meat you have from Sunday supper in with the red beans and rice. We're making ours with chicken chorizo to give it that good N'awlins spice. But, vegetarians, fret not. We've got you a big pot of red beans and smoked tofu simmering away. I think you'll like this dish boo-coo, which is Creole for "beaucoup," which means "a lot." Come and get it!

It's Tuesday. Are you hungry???

Today's lunch features Asian fare. We start with miso soup because me so in love with it. (I'm not being culturally insensitive. That's my Cookie Monster impression.)

We are also serving a bánh mi. Fun fact— did you know that the bánh mi is the only sandwich in Asia to be prepared with a European-style bread? The French lived in Asia (some might say "occupied," but bring that up with your history teacher) from 1946 to 1954. The bánh mi is a result of that culinary cross-pollination. Traditionally the protein is pork, but we make ours with glazed and roasted tofu so that it's vegetarian friendly. We toast the bread, slather on sriracha mayo, and then layer the tofu with pickled carrots, watermelon radishes, and fresh cilantro. *Bon appétit!*

Reading Chef Rooney's blog felt like getting a daily email from a friend. Which was why I was surprised when she showed up at my table. Chef Rooney was, and is, a beautiful young black woman with a mass of curly hair wound up into a bun. She was shorter than I was, with the same curvy but strong physique that my mom had. She reminded me of the Shakespeare phrase my dad always used when talking about my mother—*aunque sea poco, es poderosa*. Although she be little, she is fierce.

She reached out her hand to shake mine, and said, "Hi, I'm Rooney. A little bird told me you've been reading my blog."

I nodded. "It's really good."

"Do you want to come see how we cook in the kitchen?"

I did.

For the rest of the week, as soon as my lunch period began, I went straight to the kitchen to see Rooney and even help out. Let me qualify that by saying that in the beginning, I didn't so much help as hang out and eat. But she let me wear the chef's jacket and pulled my hair under a paper hat, because Rooney explained that the city health commissioner could pop in at any time, and Rooney would lose her job if there was even the smallest violation.

I found out that she was twenty-five and had been out of culinary school for four years. She'd studied in Paris and then had begun working in catering for movie sets, which she'd quickly found to be not as glamorous as it seemed. "But you know how the entertainment industry is—ugh." I nodded, reveling in the fact that Rooney had no idea who my mother was or what my parents did for a living.

When she asked about me, I kept it vague—grew up in Mexico City, my parents came here for work, my brother was away at school.

That Friday afternoon, I took a selfie of myself in the chef's jacket and hat that Rooney had lent me and sent the picture to Sergio with the caption, "Working hard, or hardly working?"

By dinner that night, my parents had both received the photo from Sergio, who was so clearly used to me hardly working that he'd sent it to my parents as a bat signal of how poorly I was coping with the move.

"Are you making meals at that school?" my mother wondered, distressed. "Is it a requirement that all the students work?"

My father was even more incensed. "Do they think you should cook because you're Mexican?"

"Whoa! Calm down," I told them. Way to get worked up over nothing. "The school chef has a cool blog. Her name is Rooney. She's from New Orleans. She's kind of amazing. She heard that I'd been reading her blog, so she invited me to see how she cooks. I have to wear the jacket to be in the kitchen. I like it."

My mother started muttering under her breath in Spanish, her way of coping with the fact that my father insisted we speak English at the dinner table. Then she said, "Well, I don't like it so much. You're getting ready to go to college, not cooking school."

My father, who is normally the definition of Señor Chill, was angry to the point of almost yelling. "My point exactly, Carolina. There are enough Mexicans in the kitchens of American restaurants doing the hard work."

I was in shock. "How can you say that? Would you say that—could you say that—about black people or Asian people?"

He said, "I wouldn't say it. But when it comes to Mexicans, my own people, I say what I want."

"Papá," I said. "Rooney is smart. She's fluent in French. She studied under Alain Ducasse in Paris. Someday she's going to open her own restaurant and you'll be bragging about how she was my friend."

My mother began to say something, then thought better of it. I don't know if it was the mention of Paris or Alain Ducasse, but my father seemed to have calmed down.

"Camilla, *querida*," he began, "I'm glad you have a new friend. I have the utmost respect for great chefs. I just hope you *also* make some new friends your age."

I wanted to say, "You and me both."

10

★

YOUR ACCENT IS SO CUTE!

A few weeks after I'd started hanging out with Rooney, two things happened. The first was that I started to learn how to cook. First I watched as she showed me the proper way to cut vegetables. Not so hard, I realized. Then I saw how to roast a chicken and how to make a proper Caesar salad. She explained that the Caesar salad was invented in Mexico, by the way. The other thing that happened was that I met a couple of girls who seemed like they wanted to be my friends.

"Hey, I think you're in my Tapestries class," said a girl who introduced herself as Willow.

I didn't know for sure. Tapestries was an assembly class, held in the gym. There were more than fifty kids.

"Do you work in the kitchen?" she asked.

"Not really," I explained. "But Chef Rooney is teaching me how to make a few things."

Willow didn't seem to hear the "not working" part, because she said, "Well, maybe one day when you're not working, you can have lunch with me and my friend Tiggy. She's a little OTT, but she's good people."

Rooney had been peeping the whole situation. "You should have lunch with them tomorrow. You're here to be with the other kids, not to cook."

The kitchen was open plan, which meant you could see us cooking from any of the student tables. As I was talking to Rooney, Milly, the girl with the tattoos, walked by. She looked at my cooking jacket and gave me a dirty look. "All Mexicans to the kitchen? I didn't hear the announcement."

I was so startled, I didn't know what to say, which was just as well, because she didn't stop for my response. It was just burn and roll.

I turned to Rooney. "That's what my dad said when I told him I was hanging out in the kitchen with you."

Rooney looked sympathetic. "It's tough when you're a minority to figure out what you love, as opposed to what you want to do for the mere fact of defying expectations. My dad refused to pay for me to go to culinary school. He said generations of black women had sweated and slaved to get out of the kitchen. We'd finally elected a black president, and he was accusing me of wanting to take us back to the days when women like me toiled over a hot stove."

She added, "But I fell in love with cooking, and maybe

you will too. Our history is always with us, but I think food is one of the most powerful game changers there is. We all eat. Every day. That's power. Every time you put a plate in front of someone, you are telling them a story. That's why I love doing the blog. Lookit, first let me try to get this little culinary internship approved by the administration. If your parents give their permission—and by 'permission' I mean they call me, not send a text or a possibly forged note— you can come help me on Tuesdays and Thursdays before school starts. That'll leave your lunch hours free to hang with other kids and not look like the help."

I told her it was a deal, and once my father called with his okay, it was.

★ ★ ★

The next day I had lunch with Willow and Tiggy. Willow explained that she was biracial—black mom, white dad, and as she put it, "heavily African American identified." She smiled and said, "It's like Drake said, 'Hardly home, but always repping.'"

Tiggy introduced herself as "a garden-variety white girl. Park Avenue born. Palisades raised."

"So," Willow said. "Can I ask you a question? Do a lot of Mexican girls have blond hair?"

I shook my head. "Some do. But I'm a bottle blonde."

Tiggy peered at me over her Chanel cat's-eye shades. "So what's up with that? Are you running from the law? Witness protection?"

No, I told her.

"Did you ever work as a drug mule?"

No.

Then Willow said it, "Your accent is so cute."

This may sound crazy, but I didn't think I had an accent. I speak English fluently. We all do in my family. I watch all of my favorite TV shows and movies in English. I sing along to all of my favorite songs on Google radio. When I traveled during the summer with my parents, everyone always commented on how good my English was. But alas, here it was. The thing that everyone at school kept saying was, "Oh. My. God. Your accent is so cute." It was slightly disconcerting, like discovering you have a big mole on a part of your face that you'd never seen before.

Tiggy sat staring at me, her chin propped on her hand. "I love the way you talk. It's almost like watching a foreign movie. How long have you lived in the US? Because you sound like you're fresh off the boat."

I said, in the calmest way I could, "Well, actually, we flew here."

I wanted to add, "By private plane. But whatever." I didn't. The point was to stay low-key.

Tiggy said, "Of course you flew. We didn't mean to imply that you snuck across the border, crawling on your belly, under a barbed wire. Though, I will say that's how my nanny, Cresencia, got here."

I was incredulous, and fascinated.

"So tell us how you got into Polestar in the middle of the year?" Willow asked. "The waiting list is insane, and I can't imagine there's any financial aid left at this time of year."

I thought, "Oh, I get it. Financial aid. They think I'm poor." That was interesting. I was anonymous, and now I got to ditch the whole MAP thing. Now I understood why Sergio had moved to Europe. It's easier to try on a new identity when you cross a border.

"Well, I guess I just got lucky," I said modestly.

Then Tiggy looked at me and said, "Is that T-shirt Proenza Schouler?"

Willow touched my shoulder and said, "Tiggy's parents own a boutique. She's like a living, breathing fashion encyclopedia."

My mother had offered to take me back-to-school shopping at Barneys, and I had let her because while I do not go much for makeup, I love shopping. I thought the T-shirt was understated and cool. I guess I had miscalculated. I decided to play dumb.

"Prowen who?" I said, looking confused. Maybe I was a better actress than I gave myself credit for.

Tiggy gave me a sympathetic look, then spoke to me, loudly and slowly as if I did not speak fashion fluently. "Proenza Schouler," she said. "It's okay. Cresencia's daughters wear all of my hand-me-downs too."

Willow glared at Tiggy. "Why are you assuming her mother is a domestic?"

Tiggy rolled her eyes. "Because that's what she said, right? That her mother was a maid and that she was on scholarship."

I had in fact said nothing of the kind. But my parents always told me that the first rule of improv was to agree. Just go with it. You never say no. You say, "Yes and . . ."

Willow looked to me to confirm or deny, and what I said was, "Well, it's complicated."

Both girls seemed appeased. Then Willow said, "I like the way you talk. You don't sound like most of the Mexicans in LA."

Tiggy snorted. "And how many Mexicans do you know in LA, *ése?*"

I was appalled and fascinated. It was like I'd snuck onto the set of a new TV game show, *Just How Racist Can You Be in an Hour?*

Willow said, "I was born and raised in LA. I've been around Mexicans my whole life, Tiggy."

"Oh yeah? Gardeners and maids don't count," Tiggy said defiantly. "Unless you've sat down and had a meaningful discussion with either?"

Willow linked arms with me. "Well, my new friend is a proud Mexican American, and I look forward to her teaching me everything about her culture."

Was I just Mexican, or was I Mexican American? Is that something that happened the minute you crossed the border?

I smiled weakly. I felt like Faye Dunaway in *Chinatown*. I didn't know what to think of these girls. I liked them. I hated them. I liked them.

Tiggy said, "*Our* new friend. From now on, you sit with us at lunch when you're not in the kitchen."

I looked around the cafeteria at all the kids who seemed to have known each other forever. Sure, Sergio would lump Willow and Tiggy into the same category as Patrizia. I could just hear him now, in his Oxford-tinged English saying, "What a bloody waste of space." But I liked the blank slate of not being Carolina del Valle's daughter. I liked the slightly superior feeling I had of being smarter than these girls and nowhere as racist. Sure, in Mexico City, I was a bit of a princess. Maybe I walked like one, talked like one, and God knows I shopped like one. But I would've never said half the ignorant things these girls had said to me, in less than an hour. So there was that. I didn't know where I belonged at Polestar, but you had to start somewhere.

"Thanks for the invite," I said, meaning it.

11

★

LIE TO ME

There's a science to lying. I know because my mother once
played a criminal psychologist whose specialty was help-
ing prosecutors put away hard-to-convict criminals.

So here's how to tell if someone's lying, in case you ever
really need to know:

Word repetition. Liars tend to repeat rehearsed state-
ments.

Pitch. When someone's nervous, their vocal cords
tighten and their pitch tends to go up. So you can hear their
voice get a little higher at the end of the sentence. Like
when your boyfriend says, "I'm just going out with the guys,"
but "the guys" sounds all high and squeaky, when your boyfriend's voice is never like that.

False starts. Liars tend to self-correct, so they'll start to spill the beans, and then they stop and begin again. For example, "I was on my . . . I mean, we were at the library until ten p.m., when it closed."

This is the thing. None of this would have helped Willow and Tiggy catch me, because I am what clinical psychologists refer to as a relaxed liar. I was enjoying myself. I was comfortable with my material and my audience. I didn't give any tics because the lies flowed easily and I felt good about them. Slightly psychopathic, I know.

I always knew that I would make a good liar. When your mother is an actress, you learn quickly how to pretend. As far back as I can remember, my mom's moods were a ball that she threw out and that I learned to catch and throw back. If she was happy, I was happy. If she was OMG, so excited, then I was giddy too. If she was sad or depressed, I was appropriately and sympathetically somber. It was never something we discussed, just something I did. But like most things, the more you do it, the better you get at it. By the time I got to Polestar Academy in LA, I was a pro.

I never intended to lie to Willow and Tiggy. Never planned on being a pretend *chola* girl from the barrio. It was just that when they threw it out there, I did what my instincts were honed to do. I caught their perception and tossed it back to them. Then, as if it was the most natural thing in the world, we started to play catch.

Did you know that some studies say that the average person tells three lies every ten minutes? Most are little lies to protect feelings, like, "Wow, your haircut looks great" or to cover up your screwups, like, "I can't believe I left that algebra worksheet on the kitchen table. I spent two hours on that thing!" But we all lie all day long. In fact, my mother, in her wisdom as a TV doctor, said that people who never lie, who feel the relentless compunction to tell the truth and nothing but the truth, are suffering from a kind of mental illness—one that can run the gamut from narcissistically mean and thoughtless to cold-blooded and pathologically insane. She always told me and Sergio, "When it comes down to telling a truth that would hurt my feelings or a lie that will help me be strong enough to get through the day, *mientame*, lie to me."

So when I started lying at my new school, it felt like a kindness, going along with my new friends' expectations. But it was also entertaining. Pulling one over on them made me feel like some cultural undercover crusader. The *loco* things they said made me want to laugh out loud.

★ ★ ★

Cooking with Rooney twice a week was the proverbial icing on the cake. Mexico has great food. Not just tacos and burritos but really amazing modern food. But before I started at Polestar, I'd never made anything. My mom doesn't cook. Albita made my father his favorite traditional meals, and the rest of the food was made by her personal chef Diana. In our house, meals appeared on the table three times a day, and I'd never given much thought about where they came from.

Working with Rooney was a revelation. She made a lot of Mexican dishes because, she said, "it's only natural in California to work that flavor profile." But she made things her own way: pumpkin spread on a vegetable torta, plantain empanadas, and salmon panuchos. I grew to love the quiet work of making a meal, and there was also this immediate gratification: you worked for an hour or even sometimes thirty minutes, and there was a beautiful meal—done and ready for eating. I'd always liked science, but I hadn't realized how much of cooking was scientific, how you used accelerants like heat on the grill and citrus in the seviche to transform the flavors and textures of the raw ingredients.

I hadn't read much poetry in English, but every time I stepped into Rooney's kitchen, my mind flashed to a poem by Elizabeth Alexander:

> *Science, science, science!*
> *Everything is beautiful.*
> *Elegant facts await me.*
> *Small things in this world are mine.*

★ ★ ★

Tiggy, Willow, and I were having lunch at our usual spot when Willow said, "So here's the thing. I'm barely passing Spanish."

Tiggy looked at me and explained, "By 'barely passing,' she means she's got a C, or as they put it here, SAI—Suggested Area of Improvement."

Willow looked upset. "You know that Cs aren't good enough in my house."

Tiggy replied, "I know, mine neither. But you could try to show a little sensitivity to Camilla. She's new to this country. Polestar is as competitive as hell, and English is not her first language. Chances are, she's going to end up with a few Cs on her report card this quarter."

It was interesting, how they each took turns standing up for me. They weren't mean girls exactly. More like misguided.

"Anyway," Willow continued, "my dad said he'll pay you twenty-five dollars an hour to tutor me in Spanish, two days a week."

Tiggy looked surprised and whispered, loud enough for me to hear, "That's probably more than her mother makes per hour."

That, of course, was not true. It occurred to me that this would be a good time to tell the truth. "Hey, guys, I was conducting a social experiment for psych class. My mom isn't a maid; she just plays one on TV." But I didn't want to go back to being the daughter of a television star. Even if it was a star most people in the US had never heard of, being a celebrity kid was like wearing a too-tight sports bra that you could never take off. Sure, it offered up a certain level of support, but it was also as stifling as hell.

I took a deep breath. My mother's first appearance on

99

Shot Callers wouldn't come until May sweeps. Her own show wouldn't debut until July. It was January. I had at least three or four months of keeping my secret. Maybe more, depending on how successful her show was and how much press they threw behind it.

Tiggy looked at me pityingly and then said to Willow, "See, you've insulted her."

I shrugged. "I'm not insulted. Who couldn't use some extra cash, right?"

Willow beamed. "Great. Can we start tomorrow after school?"

"Sounds good," I said. Then for extra emphasis, I added, "Will your dad pay me in cash after each tutoring session?"

Willow said, "Of course!" Then, as if I wasn't sitting right next to her, she whispered to Tiggy, "I told you. She needs the money."

I smiled broadly and stood up. "We all need money, right? How does the expression go? No shame in my game."

Willow looked relieved. "You're absolutely right. No shame in your game."

Tiggy nodded. "No shame at all."

As I walked away, I could hear Willow—who had absolutely no volume control—say, "I love her. I'm so happy that Polestar has doubled down on both racial and economic diversity."

To which Tiggy replied, "True dat, *ése*."

The next morning before I left for school, I FaceTimed Sergio. Seven a.m. for me was four p.m. for him. It was the perfect time to chat, just when my bro was feeling that midafternoon slump and craving caffeine. He made himself a cup of espresso while I talked.

"So, Camilla, how is Operation Poor Girl going?"

"Excellent. Yesterday one of the girls offered me a job tutoring her in Spanish."

"That doesn't sound bad," he said, opening two packets of Sugar in the Raw.

"It's not," I explained. "Guess how much they're paying me?"

"Ten dollars an hour?"

I beamed. "Twenty-five! Boom! My anthropological experiment continues, and I get to make some nice cheddar."

He looked concerned. "What are you going to do when those girls find out the truth about you?"

I didn't want to hear it. "They're the ones who jumped to all kinds of conclusions about me being poor and a scholarship student."

My tall, dark, and handsome brother sat back at his fancy desk and said, "When they find out the truth, your friends will be hurt."

I hadn't used those words in my mind, but I had to admit that in just a few short weeks, Tiggy and Willow had started to feel like friends. Sure, they were a little racist. But maybe we all are.

Changing the subject, I said, "The studio has hired a dialogue coach for our mother."

He laughed. "The purpose being?"

I smirked. "They want her to be able to control her accent so she can play her own American-born twin."

Then in his most flawless *Scarface* accent, Sergio said, "The accent always tells the truth, even when the rest of you is lying. Good luck with that, chief."

He smiled and then waved goodbye. *"Hasta luego,* Camilla."

I smiled back. *"Hasta luego,* Sergio."

12

★

THE GARDENER

It was lunchtime, aka Mexican Cultural Hour. It was my fault. I was the one who was lying through my teeth to my only two friends about who I was and what my family was like. So I had to take some of the blame when, holding up a pair of chopsticks as she dug into her sushi lunch, Tiggy asked me, "Hey, Camilla, did you ever date a drug dealer?"

I had been at Polestar for two months but knew that, despite the fact that tuition was four times the national average salary in Mexico, I was, in fact, surrounded by more drug dealers than I had ever been before in my life.

"Define 'drug dealer,'" I said innocently.

"You know what I mean," Tiggy said.

Willow looked annoyed. "C'mon, Antigone," she said,

using Tiggy's full name. "You're being so insensitive. Who knows what she had to do in Mexico to *survive*."

Sweet.

"What do you mean by 'drug dealer'?" I asked, looking around the room. "Do you mean like Ethan who deals E? Or the weed guy, Scott? Or someone like Wyatt, who can be counted on for the harder stuff?"

This was not only true but also a bit of a dig. Tiggy had a crazy crush on Scott Merchant, and I knew it.

Tiggy glared at me. "If you don't want to talk about your past, then just say so. I just mean, Willow and I have embraced you with open arms. We let you into our country. You got a scholarship to our school. The least you could do is exchange in a little honest dialogue."

Was she really saying that my ability to attend Polestar, live in America, and not be a social pariah at school was all because of the kindness of her little fashion-obsessed heart? She had to be kidding. Even though I knew I was escalating the drama, I said, "How about today, instead of delving into my immigrant past, we talk about you and your dirty little secrets? What were you into before I got to town? Was it anorexia, bulimia? Cutting? Shoplifting? What did you do because you're a bored little rich girl? What are you *ashamed* of?"

Both girls stared at me as if I'd just slapped Tiggy, which is sort of what I'd done. I had thought I was done with Patrizia, but every once in a while, she popped out—my inner mean girl. Or maybe I couldn't blame Patrizia at all. Maybe that's just how we're all wired, with that little sliver of ice in our hearts.

"Wow," Willow said, standing with her tray. "I think we should all take a step back and cool down. After all, we're friends."

Tiggy stood up too. Then she turned to me and said, "How about tomorrow you try not to pour so much bitch juice into your morning tequila?"

I actually laughed. "Oh, is that a Mexican joke? Hilarious." But it wasn't funny. Not at all.

I wasn't going to be able to keep it up much longer. But I wasn't sure what "it" was—my friendship with Willow and Tiggy, or the lies upon which our friendship was based.

I had thought it would be easier in America. When I lived in Mexico, it seemed like ours was almost a cartoon life. It was all a little unreal—the industry my parents were in, our gargantuan house, the staff and the security. It was as if I was always waiting for my regular life to start, the moment when I went away to school the way Sergio had, and nobody cared that my mother was famous and that our family was successful. I looked forward to being just Camilla, a girl whose BFF didn't sell her family secrets to the tabloids and who might just learn how to blend into the crowd. But maybe the truth was that I'd done a better job of blending in with the stereotypes than blending into any crowd.

The LA Camilla was closer to the girl I'd always felt I was on the inside. Our house in Beverly Hills was nice, but it wasn't a crazy blinged-out compound like our place back home. Albita still lived with us—I don't think my mother could manage without her—but none of the other staff members did. My mother went to the gym instead of having a trainer come to the house. The drivers and the cleaning people and the organic chef came in and out, but they didn't live with us the way they had in Mexico. I was taking the bus to school—the bus!

Sergio encouraged me to go out for some school activities. "You're going to have to meet some other kids when this Camilla from the Barrio act comes crashing down." I knew he was right. Not to mention that my college counselor said my grades were good for an "international" student but every university wants their students to be well rounded. I thought I might try out for the tennis team in the spring. I wasn't that good, but I loved to play. It might have been all the *Law & Order* episodes I'd been binge-watching since we'd moved to the US, but I was also thinking about going out for mock trial in the fall.

Then of course, there was the little one-woman show I'd been putting on for Willow and Tiggy. You'd think it would be some sort of sign that the gift of acting had been passed down to me. But I don't think you can call it acting when the lines practically write themselves.

The next day, after Tiggy and I had mumbled our apologies, we managed to spend almost the entire lunch hour without talk delving into Mexican Culture: Fact, Fiction, and Fantasy. Then Willow had to go there.

"So your mother's a maid, right?" she began.

"That's what the uniform says," I answered.

Tiny lie.

"And what does your dad do?" she asked.

I tried to stay as close to the truth as possible. "He's been looking for work," I said. "But these days, he's been spending most of his time in the garden."

This was not a lie. While my mother was off to the studio every day and had a full schedule of meetings with producers, sessions with her new American acting coach, and of course lots of Pilates and lots of shopping, my father was not as busy. He had an agent, but there wasn't as much voice-over work for a Spanish-speaking actor in Los Angeles as there was in Mexico City. Most of that work in the US was based in Miami. So my father had turned all Edward Scissorhands in our garden. It was beautiful and a little haunting.

Willow looked sympathetic. "I see those guys on the side of the road all the time, hoping to get picked up for day work."

I nodded. I'd seen them too. Was I going straight to hell for my lies?

That evening, after our Spanish tutoring session, Willow handed me seventy-five dollars for three hours of tutoring. She then added a crisp hundred-dollar bill to the small stack.

"What's this?" I asked, handing it back to her.

"It's a bonus," she said, pushing the money back toward me. "I got a B-plus on my Spanish vocab quiz, and Señorita Gomez said that my accent has vastly improved."

I tried to give her the hundred back. "That's because you've been studying your ass off. That's you. Not me."

"Keep it," Willow said. "And if you ever need money, a loan, anything, you just ask."

I was touched. I couldn't remember ever making an offer like that to a friend. But then again, in Mexico, I didn't have any friends whose families weren't affluent. And I'd never given it a second thought. I tucked the extra money into my wallet because I knew she wanted me to have it.

Just when I thought Willow could not have been any kinder, she hugged me. "We girls of color have got to stick together," she said.

It was so unexpected. I always thought of them as a twosome—Willow and Tiggy. Tiggy and Willow. But I could count on my hands the number of brown girls in our grade at Polestar. Willow was so wealthy and so fabulous, it had never occurred to me that she might feel like an outsider. I guess I knew now what my classmates had thought about me back home.

As I did every time I left Willow's house, I walked down to the bus stop on Wilshire. Then I called an Uber. The school bus was cool, but I wasn't looking to ride a city bus from Hancock Park to Beverly Hills. As I slid into the back of the town car, all I could think was that I really hoped Willow would still be my friend when I told her the truth, which would be soon-ish.

When I got home, my father was in the backyard weeding—weeding or planting. I honestly knew so little about gardening that I couldn't tell the difference. So I asked him.

He was dressed in a pair of denim overalls and a khaki button-down shirt. If my friends from Polestar could've seen him, they would have mistaken him for a day worker looking for landscaping work, or even a migrant worker. How did that saying go? Clothes maketh the man?

My father told me that he was planting for spring. "We're going to have a beautiful garden come May," he said. "These are actually for you."

He held up a packet of seeds. Camellia roses. So sweet.

I kissed him on the forehead. "Thank you, Papá."

"You're welcome, *niña*," he said. "Your mother is out at an event tonight. It's just you and me for dinner. I was thinking we should go out."

It crossed my mind that I might cook for my dad, but I had no idea if we had the ingredients. I quickly agreed. "For burgers and fries?" I asked hopefully.

"Lots and lots of fries," he said. "Just let me shower and change."

Driving down the LA side streets with my father, I loved how empty they were. It was a little after eight. The evening traffic had died down and the city was quiet, at least on our side of town. It was all palm trees and streetlights and that bright blue haze of a sky above us.

"So where are we going?" I asked.

"You'll see," my father said with a smile.

A few minutes later, we pulled in front of a place called Father's Office. I burst out laughing.

As we took our seats, my father said, "So although you should not skip school, if you do, then meet me—this is our spot. You can say, 'I've got an emergency and I've got to go to my father's office.' "

I smiled. "Really? I can cut school and meet you here?"

"*Sí*," my father said. Then he shook his head. "No."

"Which one is it?"

"Maybe every once in a while."

Once we'd devoured our burgers, I asked him the difficult, delicate question for out-of-work actors. "So how's the auditioning going?"

He smiled. "Good news, actually. I booked a part."

"Really? Way to go!" I said, clinking my soda bottle with his pint of beer. "What is it?"

"Robot Number Three in an action flick," he said. "It's only two lines. But it's in English, so it's a start. You know what they say: *del suelo no paso.*" You can't fall down from the floor. In other words, there's nowhere to go but up. I was happy for my father. He was starting a new chapter too. What I hoped, more than anything I wished for myself, was that my dad would get his own shine here in the US, that he wouldn't just be Mr. Carolina del Valle.

At every awards show my mother was ever honored at, she thanked my father for being *el viento bajo mis alas,* the wind beneath her wings. But take it from me, if you ever get the choice between being the wind or being the one with wings, choose wings. Being the wind sucks.

★ ★ ★

A couple of weeks later, my dad got a bigger gig—a Spanish voice-over for the new Iron Man movie. He was going to be playing Iron Man, which meant weeks and weeks of work. They even flew in his favorite producer, Rogelio Claro, from Mexico to work on the project.

His first night in town Rogelio came over for dinner.

"Ay, *chica*, you're even taller than the last time I saw you!" he said, giving me a hug when I opened the front door.

"That was just three months ago, Tío," I said. We call all of our parents' close friends "aunt" or "uncle."

He shrugged. "You're taller. It's the American way. Supersize me, am I right?"

My father came in and gave Rogelio the Mexican man half hug, half handshake. "*Hombre, qué pasa?*"

Then my mother came in, and Rogelio lifted her off the ground and spun her around. "*Corazón!* It's the American movie star," he said.

My mother blushed. "TV," she said. "And not star. Not films. Not yet."

It was the first time we were entertaining a guest from home, and we were all positively giddy. By the end of the evening, Rogelio was dancing with Albita and my father was twirling my mother around the patio. I thought about Amadeo and the whole crazy way that I'd met him. Our love story was almost like a telenovela. But was it real? Would it last? I was more unsure than I'd ever been. I watched my parents for a moment from the staircase, remembering all the parties they'd thrown in Mexico. Then I tiptoed up to bed.

That Friday, after school, I went to visit my father at the studio in Culver City where he and Rogelio were working. The recording studios for voice-overs were light-years away from the television studios. There was no big security booth, just a guy in a uniform at a desk who would have *preferred* that I show him a form of ID. But when I told him that I didn't have one, he said, "Okay, fine, just sign your name here." Then, as if this was a deterrent, he added, "Your *real* name."

I took the elevator to the fifth floor of what looked like a regular office building, found the suite I was looking for, and walked in. It was just my father, Rogelio, and a sound engineer inside.

The movie was playing on a screen on the far wall of the studio, and my father sat on a high chair in the soundproof booth, wearing a pair of headphones and holding a script. He waved at me when I came in.

I quietly took a seat behind the sound engineer, pulled out my chemistry homework, and watched my dad do his thing.

"I'm a huge fan of the way you lose control and turn into an enormous green rage monster."

"You know, it's times like this, I realize what a huge superhero I am."

I did my best not to burst out laughing. But he was so funny, so charming. I thought, one day, people will know how amazing my father is. One day, it will all come out. One year for Christmas, Sergio got my dad a T-shirt that said GET THE MONEY, F*** THE FAME. My bro had explained to me that although my father wasn't as well known as our mother, he was—in his own right—very successful. "None of this would go away if Mami stopped working," Sergio said. "Dad could cover it all—the house, our school tuition, maybe a little less staff, but we'd be fine. It's important that he knows that we're proud of him, that we see all that he does for us, because while it seems like this is the Carolina del Valle show at home, it's not."

"I see you, Papi," I wanted to say through the sound-proof glass that separated me from my father. "And there's no place I'd rather be than right here with you." No cast of thousands. No wind machines. No hair, no makeup, no sequins. Just my dad's voice, Rogelio's sotto voce comments, and a movie that hadn't even opened in the theaters yet, playing on silent, on the screen in front of me. Heaven.

13

★

THE FRONT THIRTEEN

In some ways my mother's life, at least schedule-wise, was the same. She got up early for her morning ritual of running on the treadmill, followed by a big glass of juice. While my father and I were just stumbling into the kitchen for our morning *cafecito*, she was dressed and headed out the door. She kissed each of us and yelled, *"Es un buen día pa tener un buen día."* It's a good day to have a good day. Each morning, the studio sent a car to pick her up, and she had fallen into an easy rapport with Ilías, her new driver. It took thirty or forty minutes to get to the studio, time my mother spent learning her lines and playing with her new favorite app, Duolingo. "I thought my English was pretty good," she said in her throaty, movie-star voice. "But it's like my *abuela* always said, 'See me' and 'Come live with me' are two entirely different things. As a tourist, my English is perfect. As a resident, not so much."

I was also settling into the fact that this was more than an extended vacation. Los Angeles was our home now. "Do you miss home?" my father sometimes asked me. Yes, I missed the place—hearing everyone speak Spanish the way that I spoke it. In the US, everyone's Spanish is different. Mexican Spanish is different from Mexican American Spanish; the way Nicaraguans speak is different from how a Cuban or a Colombian might speak. Of course, I heard different Latin accents at home, but I hadn't recognized how much you grow accustomed to the hum of your own language, how much it makes you feel at home to walk into any room, or turn on the radio or the TV, and understand exactly what is being said. My English was good, maybe stronger than my parents' even, but a dozen times a day or more, I had to ask someone to repeat him or herself. "Hmm, what did you say?" In class, if I daydreamed for even five minutes, I would lose the thread and have to pay super-close attention just to pick up the subject. I liked the challenge of it. Maybe because I had watched my brother master English while at boarding school and then had seen him pick up German at the university, but I had begun to think of being bilingual as one of my superpowers. I wasn't super-pretty or rocket-scientist smart, but there were now two of me—the girl I was in Spanish and the girl I was becoming in English, and

I liked the fact that each of my selves had her own language, her own way of hearing and being heard in the world.

My father, I think, missed Mexico most of all. My mother had been the star there, but her celebrity had limited her. There were so many places she couldn't go and things she couldn't do. She was like this rare beautiful bird and our home had been her cage. As a voice-over actor, my father had suffered no such restriction. He loved Mexico City and he loved showing it off. Even when my mother's success meant that we might be targets for kidnapping, my father would pile me into the car with security, and we'd go driving around the *colonias*. He would pull up pictures on his iPad and show me how Mexico City's main boulevard, the Paseo de la Reforma, was so much like Paris's famous Champs-Élysées. He'd show me pictures of Gaudí architecture in Barcelona and the slickly designed art mecca of Bilbao as we drove through the streets of Colonia Cuauhtémoc. It was my father who took me on annual pilgrimages to Frida Kahlo and Diego Rivera's Casa Azul every July 6, on Frida's birthday. And then there was the food.

My mother was always watching her weight, so even if she could have hit up every dive bar and café in La Roma, she wouldn't. But my father loved to eat, and drink, and there wasn't a restaurant we visited where the owners didn't know him by name. From the high-end molecular gastronomy restaurants where the olives dissolved into briny liquid the minute you bit into them, to the most humble torta stands and *loncherías*, my father knew them all.

Sometimes we were joined by my father's friends from

the world of voice-overs: Rogelio, his favorite producer; Sammy, the sound guy; and other actors like Bobby and Hector. Bobby was a big guy with a belly like Santa Claus's and a booming laugh. Hector was the opposite, tall and skinny, with hair that was always a little too long and with what my dad liked to call a "villain's mustache."

Sometimes it was just the two of us; sometimes we rolled around in a giant SUV, picking up members of my father's crew before taking off to some magnificent place to eat.

My father liked the hidden places best—the places that didn't have a sign out front or any indication that beyond those doors lay some of the most delicious food you ever tasted. I can close my eyes and be back there, in the garden of Los Chicos Chapultepec. To get to the Chicos, you have to walk through an antiques store that looks like your grand-mother's attic that hadn't been cleaned out in decades. But in the back, there was Jago, manning the grill, serving up the most delicious tortas on his mother's homemade bread—grilled octopus, short ribs with red chile sauce, chicken marinated with red onions. I mean, *heaven.*

Then there was Salvatore's, my father's favorite barber-shop. You had to climb three flights of stairs in an old nineteenth-century building, but when you got to the top floor, you reached this beautiful loft, with midcentury mod-ern furniture, everything slick and smooth like something out of *Architectural Digest.*

In one corner, there were two vintage barber chairs. On the far side of the room, there was a long banquette where Crista, Salvatore's girlfriend, served up tapas and tonics.

This was my father's world, a whole city of places where he was known and loved and treated like a king. It was good that he had his Iron Man movie to voice over. It was nice that Rogelio Claro, his buddy, had come to town and the studio had rented Rogelio an apartment in the Wilshire district, just a fifteen-minute drive away. But Mexico City was a booming metropolis that my father knew *como la palma de su mano*, like the palm of his hand. Los Angeles was still, for him, a city of closed doors, and I knew that he sometimes felt like he would never see more than the back of Hollywood's hand.

My mother's show had received an order for what they call the front thirteen. Telenovelas are actually something between an American TV series and a series of movies. They tend to run, from beginning to end, every week for a year, and then the whole story line is complete. That show goes away, the characters go away, and a new telenovela starts. In the US, a show can go on for years and years, but each year you get, on average, about twenty-two episodes. When a show is new and they don't know yet if it will be a hit, they order only thirteen episodes, aka "the front thirteen." The idea was that the thirteen episodes offered some sort of resolution, so even if the show was canceled, all the people who actually did watch it could be satisfied that the characters they'd invested in had a little bit of a happy ending.

By the time we'd been in the US for a few months, it was like we were at that same, "Okay, so are they going to make it or not?" point. My mother seemed to be totally not stressed about work. As far as our family was concerned, she had it the easiest. She was like a college student studying abroad. The scenery was different, but her job—stay slim and sexy, learn her lines, and perform on camera—was much the same.

Even though my dad had a job, I could tell that he missed his life in Mexico City. That was his town, and he loved rolling up to restaurants and barbershops, cigar bars, and clubs like El Colmillo, with a posse of friends in tow and old friends waiting inside. Having Rogelio around helped, but it wasn't the same. More and more, my dad complained about what he called "low hum racism"—nothing so big that it caused irreparable harm, nothing so epic that you wanted to file a case with La Raza, but incidents that messed with the general quality of your life, like interference on the radio when you're jamming out to your favorite song, or the weird warp you get sometimes when you record a show in HD and the cable is being funky. For example, one night my father and Rogelio went out to a fancy tequila tasting. This asshole pulled up in a Jag and thought my father was the valet.

"Be careful not to scratch it," the guy said, tossing my father the keys. "And no joy rides."

My father said the guy was gone before he could even explain that he didn't work there.

The actual valets, though, were peeping the whole thing and said, "Welcome to being brown in LA, *hermano*," slapping my father on the back.

It wasn't the end of the world, but still, my father said

that it had been like a gnat flying around inside his head all night. No matter how many sips of five-hundred-dollar tequila he drank, the gnat wouldn't go away.

★ ★ ★

At sixteen, I was too young to drive, and Uber was my lifeline in Los Angeles. I depended on it to take me to Willow's house for tutoring sessions and to the Grove, the outdoor shopping center where Willow and Tiggy liked to hang. I did not tell them that I Ubered it everywhere. I lied and said I took the bus—everyone knew that the LA bus system was outdated, draconian, and borderline dangerous. All I had to say was "I'll take the bus" to feel the warm blanket of sympathy thrown over me.

"Poor you," Willow would coo. "I mean, the struggle is real."

"You are a braver woman than me," Tiggy would intone, her voice filled with admiration. As a now bona fide, semi-full-time liar, I kept my stories about the bus vague, making broad allusions to the Wilshire line, or changing on well-known streets like La Brea and Fairfax. Sure, sometimes I thought, "It is ridiculous that I walk three blocks away, hide behind a shrub, and call a town car to come get me." But there was something vaguely spylike in the measures I took to protect my story, and what can I say, I was a kid who loved Nancy Drew.

The girls never asked me where I lived, exactly, or to

come over to my house. Sometimes I found myself being a little offended, and I thought, "Why don't you ever come over to my house?" Then I remembered that even if I'd wanted to, I could not invite them, because they did not expect me to live in a 1927 Spanish colonial with a pool and a guesthouse in the 90210. Hanging at my house would mean game over.

And yet, the more I lied to them, the more I discovered things about them that really touched me. One afternoon we were having an after-school chowdown at Blue Ribbon Sushi at the Grove.

I tried to eat only an appetizer, figuring that even a fourteen-dollar appetizer would be a lot for a girl like the one I was pretending to be. Willow noticed right away and ordered twice as much food as she could possibly eat. She kept pushing plates toward me and saying, "Hey, Cam, try this." Or "OMG, this kanpachi with yuzu pepper is *amazing*. You've got to have some."

Then when the bill came, Tiggy grabbed it and said, "It's on me." Willow tried to take it from her and said, "Nope, my treat." And it was a little bit of a scene, the two of them fighting over the check until finally they agreed to split it.

I said, "Let me at least leave the tip. I insist. I've got money from my weekend babysitting job."

Did I mention that I'd made up an imaginary babysitting job with an imaginary kid named Benicio? Really, I was the worst.

Willow finally agreed to let me tip, and I reached into

my purse to pull out a crinkled twenty. (I spent a lot of time distressing the bills my dad gave me. For whatever reason, I thought if I was poor, my money wouldn't be crispy and new.)

Then it happened. My AmEx black card fell out of my wallet. I grabbed it quickly, but Willow noticed it right away.

"Is that a black card?" she asked, her eyes wide.

"This?" I said. "Are you kidding?"

Tiggy motioned for me to hand it over, but I refused.

"I'm actually embarrassed," I said, putting it back into my wallet. "I've been listening to a lot of motivational podcasts, and on one, this guy suggested that in order to be wealthy someday, you have to do creative visualizations. So I ordered this fake credit card online. I just wanted to imagine myself having all the money I could possibly need."

Willow started to tear up. "I think that's really wonderful, Camilla. What a positive way to approach your situation."

I was the worst. *Lo peor.*

Tiggy, however, was unimpressed. "I'm really sorry to tell you, but I don't think that positive-thinking stuff works. But you're at Polestar. You'll go to a good college. You'll be solidly upper middle class one day. That's something."

Willow glared at her. "Wow, Tiggy. Way to be condescending and classist in five sentences or less."

"I'm just speaking truth to power," Tiggy said.

"It's okay," I told Willow. "I have faith in my dreams."

That afternoon, as I waited at the bus stop for them to be far enough out of range so I could call an Uber, I told myself it wasn't bad that they treated me all the time. It's not like they couldn't afford it. "They buy me food because I'm offering a service," I thought. "I've constructed this identity, Camilla the Poor, and each day, I improvise the script like I'm starring in my own high school telenovela." When I made Tiggy laugh or I saw Willow puff up with pride at how much her Spanish was improving, I thought, "This is working." My *show* was working. My mother was not the only one with an order for the front thirteen.

14

★

THE LOVE INTEREST

Before we moved to California, I thought I was fluent in English. But in reality, I'd based this belief almost entirely on my ability to watch American movies and TV shows without subtitles and still keep up. Going to school in English—a competitive college prep school (progressive was more a "theory" than a reality)—was another thing entirely. Subjects that used to be easy for me, like history and literature, were all of a sudden hella hard.

I signed up for a class called Experimental Fiction, thinking it would be the magical realism authors that I loved, such as Gabriel García Márquez, Jorge Luis Borges, and Isabel Allende. None of those authors were on the syllabus for Experimental Fiction. That course focused on one book. It was a book about war, and I just didn't get it. Every afternoon after school, I tried to be disciplined. I plopped myself at the kitchen table with my Spanish-English dictionary. (Sergio insisted that Google Translate was an unhelpful crutch when it came to academic work.) I vowed to devote an hour a day to the book. Most days I made it twenty minutes. Occasionally I made it forty minutes, but only when I ate a ton of candy, drank soda, and let myself be hopped up on sugar. Regardless, not once did I ever make it the whole hour. Every study session ended the same, with me banging my head on the table, murmuring, *"No se puedo. No se puedo."* I just can't.

If Polestar had been any other school, I would've failed the class. Instead, because of the progressive nature of the school, my teacher marked me as IM—Improvement Made, or about a B-minus. I joked with Sergio that *IM* actually stood for "Insane Mexican" because that was what I felt like the whole time I tried to read that book.

Like so many immigrants, I discovered that while I had a way with words in my own country, getting those words down on paper was a challenge in my new home. Math and science quickly became the domains where I could shine, which was why I was psyched when my counselor announced that I was being moved from regular chemistry to honors chemistry.

This turned out to be a bit of a mixed bag. I was happy to get called off the bench for honors chemistry. Then I saw her in the class, the Mexican-looking girl with the tattoos, and I think I actually shuddered.

The upside was that the honors chemistry teacher was a fantastical man named Mr. Agrabal. Unlike most of the other teachers at Polestar, he did not want us to address him by his first name. We called him Mr. Agrabal and he, in turn, called us by our surnames. He referred to me as Ms. del Valle, which made me feel grown-up. I liked it.

Mr. Agrabal dressed in a stunning array of perfectly pressed suits. My favorite was a purple suit with a peacock-blue shirt and bright blue paisley tie. But his suits ranged in color from robin's-egg blue to sunset coral and everything in between. He seemed intent on teaching anything but chemistry. But I loved his class because he reminded me of my mother. You could tell that he loved life and he saw everything in that "bright lights, big city" way.

One afternoon, Mr. Agrabal said, "Pop quiz. How many people in this room are lactose intolerant?"

Three people raised their hands. He went over to each and squeezed their hands in his own. "My brothers and sisters in the struggle. I feel your pain. We live in California, a cheese lover's paradise. But for those of us who suffer from this dreaded disease, temptation is only dwarfed by the gargantuan reality of the suffering that will follow."

Meghan, a pretty girl with a long face that looked like it should be in a Modigliani painting, raised her hand. She said, "I eat cheese. I just take a pill."

Mr. Agrabal shook his head and clucked softly under his breath as if he were consoling a crying child. "Perhaps because you are young and American born, these pills work for you. But for me, there is no cure. I must stay away from the cheese."

Liam Baker, a tall, skinny kid with shoulder-length curly hair, raised his hand and asked, "I'm sorry, but what does any of this have to do with organic chemistry?"

Mr. Agrabal spun around and shot him the most withering glare. I half expected a wand to magically appear in Mr. Agrabal's hand and for the walls to shake, as if he was a character from Harry Potter. He was *that* wizardly.

"Cheese is organic chemistry, Mr. Baker," Mr. Agrabal growled. "Or are you not using your brain? More important, science is *useless* without the element of human compassion. Or are you not familiar with a little invention called the atom bomb?"

Liam rolled his eyes. "Sure. But we pay a lot of money to come to this school. I want to learn something useful."

At this point, I physically gasped. Back home in Mexico, no one would ever talk to a teacher that way. Not even loudmouthed Patrizia. At my school in Mexico, the men wore suits and the women wore crisp, starched cotton shirtdresses in shades of white, navy, or charcoal gray. I did not know their first names, where they lived, what they liked to eat. What they taught us seemed so prescribed, so mandated from up on high, that I never questioned where the lessons came from or how we might deviate from them.

I didn't even notice that anyone had noticed my reaction, but Mr. Agrabal came running over to me. "You," he said, pointing at me as if he were wielding a sorting hat. "Compassion. I heard it. Stand up. *Rise up!*"

I stood nervously. "To the board, Ms. del Valle. You will help me document the bounty of cheeses available in the western region of these United States."

He then pointed to Liam. "And you will write me a twenty-page double-spaced paper about the invention of the atom bomb and the push and pull between the compassionately minded members of the scientific community and how they struggled against the political ambitions of the governments they served."

Liam looked stunned. "Are you kidding me? Due when?"

Mr. Agrabal said, "Due Monday."

Liam pushed his desk away, steamed. "No way. My family's going to our house in Jackson Hole this weekend. I can't do it."

For me, it was like watching a telenovela come to life. Who talked to a teacher that way?

Mr. Agrabal took the chalk and wrote on the board "#firstworldproblems."

Liam groaned, "You're insane."

My mouth just hung open. How could he talk that way to the authority figure in the room?

Mr. Agrabal just smiled. "Let compassion be your polestar, Mr. Baker, or I will have you write another twenty-page paper on the power dynamics between humanitarians and their scientific allies and the political powers that agitated the rise of the nuclear bomb."

Liam put his head on the desk and began to bang it slowly.

"Very dramatic, Mr. Baker. Are you planning to major in theater?" Mr. Agrabal asked, grinning. "Someone let me know if he draws blood, and we'll call the school physician.

"Ms. del Valle!"

"Yes, sir," I said.

"To the board!" he said, handing me the chalk. "Let's talk cheese." He looked practically ecstatic, like my mother when her stylist came in with a Louis Vuitton trunk full of just-off-the-runway, not-yet-in-stores clothing.

"What is your favorite kind of cheese, dear?" he asked.

I thought about it, then answered, "Cotija."

He said the word again, as if he could taste it just by pronouncing it. "Cotija. Amazing. Tell me more about this cheese."

"It's a Mexican cheese . . . ," I began nervously. The whole class was staring at us, and I wasn't used to being on-stage. "It's named after the town where it was first made, Cotija, which is in a part of Mexico called Michoacán."

"Fascinating!" Mr. Agrabal said. "And what are its properties?"

"It's a crumbly, white cheese. Salty, like feta."

"It sounds scrumptious," Mr. Agrabal said, feasting on my words.

"When it ages, it gets hard and takes on a quality like Parmesan."

"And how do you serve it?"

In an instant, I was transported back to our kitchen in

Mexico. Albita was standing at the counter, grating Cotija over our dinner salad.

"You can grate it over a salad. Or you can sprinkle it on a taco. It's also good in soup."

"Splendid!" Mr. Agrabal cheered. "Write it on the board."

And that is what I did for the next forty-five minutes. I wrote the names of cheeses and their properties on the board. Cotija. Gruyère. Manchego. Cheddar. Vermont cheddar. White Cheddar. Colby. Colby Jack. Brie. It was crazy, but it was fun. Liam was wrong. It was an education. An education in life.

I left the class almost giddy. I couldn't wait to get home and give Sergio my daily report. I'd just come out of that crazy chemistry class when the cutest boy in the world came up to me. He said, "I don't think we've met. I'm white Max."

What I thought was: "I must be having one of those moments." Sometimes when I was tired, my brain got lazy and didn't translate properly.

What I said was: "I'm sorry, can you repeat that?"

"Ever since kindergarten, there were two Maxes at Polestar," he said. "They always called the other guy 'black Max.' Then around seventh grade, I kinda got woke, and I realized that was ridiculous. So I insisted that everyone call me 'white Max' so the other Max wasn't the only one being identified by his race. Black Max transferred last year to Crossroads, but by now, it's kinda stuck. Everyone calls me 'white Max.'"

"That's weird, right?" I said. It was a conversation that

intrigued me because ever since I'd moved to Los Angeles, I'd been distinctly aware that I was not white. In Mexico, I knew that everyone was a mix, to some degree, of indigenous people, European settlers, and other immigrant groups. It was something strange, but something I knew I was going to have to get used to. In Mexico, if someone had Indian or African heritage, they were called moreno or occasionally pardo—though that was a term used mostly by Brazilians. I never thought, "I'm white." But since we'd moved to the US, I'd come to think that not having to think about skin color was a way of being white—regardless of your skin color. In America, and in Los Angeles specifically, if you were Mexican, you were "brown"—no matter how white your skin was. Whiteness, I came to understand pretty quickly, was something you were given—like a passport or a green card. It wasn't actually a visual reality.

White Max smiled at me and said, "Hey, so I hear you tutor people in Spanish?"

I wanted to say yes, but I shook my head. "Yes. I mean no."

He laughed, and when he did, his eyes crinkled in a way that made me want to kiss him, just to see him smile again. "Well, which is it? Yes or no?"

I thought of Amadeo, in the basement of the university dissecting cadavers, and I felt guilty. But it seemed more and more that there were two of me. One was the Camilla I had been in the DF: serious, sure, a little cynical and sarcastic. Then there was the me who had emerged in the US: a little shady, far more opinionated, way more willing to go out on a limb just to see how far I could go. And the American me cooked. Of all the things I'd heard about immigrating to the US, I'd never thought that schizophrenia would be one of the side effects.

I stuttered. I never stuttered. "Um, well, I do tutor. But I'm kind of booked up right now."

He looked disappointed. "I'm sorry to hear that. I could really use the help in Spanish. And I wouldn't mind spending some time with you."

There it was—pure, unadulterated flirting. But that was the thing. I couldn't tutor him. I couldn't hang out with him. Because I felt, in an instant, that I couldn't lie to him. I couldn't sit there and feed him the *bochinche* that I made up like I was a character in a telenovela, some crazy amnesiac who spouts untruth after untruth because of the knock she's taken to her head.

★ ★ ★

I thought about him again that night, tried to imagine how an innocent tutoring session might lead to a kiss, which was crazy because technically I had a boyfriend. But we were on a break. And it seemed to me that if you did not at least kiss another person during such breaks, then what was the point? In *Twenty-One Love Poems*, the poet Adrienne Rich calls a prospective paramour "a prize one could wreck one's peace for." Max was like that. I would wreck my peace for him, wreck this crazy patchwork of lies that I'd put together and called my American self. I could do it, tell the truth and bear the wrath of Willow and Tiggy if he might like me and date me. It would be a relief maybe just to be the new girl, Cammi from the DF. But I was DF—definitely f***ed because Willow and Tiggy wouldn't just keep it to themselves. They'd make sure that everyone knew that I'd pretended to be cool and hood, when I was just good old Hollywood spawn.

I was picturing us laughing and having a good time when it occurred to me that what was missing from the equation was my mother. Without my mother and her fame in the mix, there was so much air. I could finally just be me.

Don't say it.

Because I already know.

"Me just being me" involved copious hours of me just being a crazy liar.

Don't think I don't know.

15

★

TRANQUILA, CHICA,
YOUR SECRET'S SAFE WITH ME

Mr. Agrabal told us that as a child, he'd dreamed of being an actor, but his father had insisted that he "pursue the lamp of learning, not the bright lights of the stage." Every Friday afternoon, Mr. Agrabal closed the shades of his classroom, pulled down the screen, and showed us forty-five minutes of a Bollywood movie. He told us that "the pursuit of true love is the most important chemical equation you will ever solve. In this manner, the instruction in these films will serve you well."

Bollywood Fridays quickly became the highlight of my week. I fell in love with the over-the-top story lines so much, like the novelas I'd grown up with. I loved the critique of colonialism of the cricket-playing Indians in *Lagaan.* In *Dil-*

wale Dulhania Le Jayenge, the Swiss mountain setting of two Indian kids falling in love on the slopes made me think of Sergio. I couldn't wait to show it to him to see if he recognized any of the places, or if it reminded him of any of his friends and the girls they chased.

A lot of us wanted to petition the school to have Mr. Agrabal teach a film class instead of chemistry. But this, he insisted, was "not a wise idea." Then he showed us the montage he'd created in which he'd Photoshopped himself into a dozen pictures of Aishwarya Rai Bachchan, one of the most famous Bollywood actresses in the world. "I think she's stalking me," Mr. Agrabal said with a grin.

As part of our midterm project, Mr. Agrabal assigned us lab partners. Because life was perfect and fair, I got assigned to the one girl at Polestar who seemed to have hated me on sight.

"Hi, I'm Camilla," I said.

She didn't look up from her notebook. "I know who you are."

I thought maybe if I spoke to her in Spanish, I might get some authenticity points, so I said, *"Así vas a decirme su nombre, o sólo va a tener yo estoy aquí como un idiota."*

Which translated meant "Are you going to tell me your name or have me just standing here like an idiot?"

She looked up finally and said, "If the shoe fits."

I asked her, *"Por qué eres tan mal educación?"*

She glared at me and said, "Don't speak to me in Spanish. You don't know me like that."

I kept talking to her in Spanish because, well, I'm a little sister. When I figure out that something is annoying you, I'm liable to keep it up. "Well, you've decided that you hate me when you don't even know me like that."

"Because those girls you hang with are mad dumb," Milly said after we'd introduced ourselves. "I've known who you were from jump."

"How?" I asked.

"I can read."

She took out a copy of *People en Español* that I had totally missed. The headline read:

Carolina del Valle Coming to America!

Rumor has it that Carolina del Valle is eyeing a move to Hollywood and has taken up residence in a quiet cul-de-sac in the Los Angeles neighborhood of Brentwood . . .

"It's Beverly Hills, not Brentwood, but whatever," I mumbled.

Distraught over the love of her life, Ivan Sancocho, Carolina says, "I just want my daughter to have a normal life."

And there it was, the photo that would never go away. Me, age eight, in a sparkling sequined one-shoulder jumpsuit at my one and only gymnastics competition. Staring at the vault like the torture device I knew it was, I look like a little bushy-eyebrowed demon.

"Nice photo," Milly said, grinning.

I kept speaking to her in Spanish. "Can you please put that away?"

"Tranquila, chica," she said. "Your secret's safe with me."

"Thank you," I said. "But why aren't you busting me if you know?"

She shot me the iciest stare that I'd ever seen, and my mother is a telenovela actress. "Because I don't care. Busting you would imply that I think you are anything more than a waste of space."

"Fine. *Gracias*. You're pretty, you know. Despite all the tattoos. You should enter a beauty contest, one that gives points for personality. Miss Congeniality."

If she was going to treat me like a "waste of space," then I was going to speak to her in Spanish and make sarcastic comments all class long.

She looked up at me and said, "Stop yapping, Chihuahua. We've got work to do."

★ ★ ★

I was shocked that chemistry became my favorite subject. Mr. Agrabal was hilarious, and as for Milly the Monster, despite the fact that she hated me, I kind of liked her. It was actually relaxing to be around someone who knew the truth about me. It was *great* to spend an hour every school day with someone who spoke my language, even if she only answered me with insults, burns, and barbs. I didn't even mind that she called me Chihuahua, because when I got to speak Spanish to someone who actually understood every word that I said, I was like an excited little puppy. I never realized how much I missed home until I got assigned to be lab partners with Milly. I loved that she understood everything I said and where I was from, but at the same time, she totally was someone I would have never met at home. One day, I just said to her—in Spanish, of course—"You know we're going to be friends, so you might as well stop fighting it."

She looked at me seriously and said, "I don't want to be friends if that means you'll be lying to me like you lie to your other so-called friends. Come clean with those *chicas*, and you and me can hang."

I felt my whole face go red. "Well, I'm a little deep into it right now."

"So when do you plan on fessing up?"

I said, "Summer vacation. I'll send them an e-greeting."

"Not cool, Camilla," she said.

"Why do you care?" I asked. "They're just a bunch of *tontas*."

She looked at me, and for once she didn't seem angry or annoyed. She just seemed real. "The life you're pretending to have is real to people like me. Do you watch the news? Are you paying attention to this election? We have a bunch of right-wing lunatics who want to make it impossible for all the undocumented kids who were *born* here to go to college and improve their lives. You're an educated Mexican who came here with buckets of cash. You could change the minds of kids at this school who think we're all one stereotype after another. Maybe those same kids would go home and talk to their parents. The parents at this school have *influence*. They get it done. But instead of being a force for good, you're fake slumming it and perpetuating stereotypes. So we can't be friends until you kill that noise."

I wanted to. I knew it was time. So I started in the place where I felt safest of all—the kitchen.

I'd never lied to Rooney. It had been more a sin of omission. Because I'd fallen in love with cooking and Rooney was the person I admired most at Polestar, I figured that telling her about my family was a good start.

One morning, early before school started, we were prepping Cuban sandwiches for the afternoon lunch. We laid out each ingredient, chopped and ready to go, so every sandwich would be ready to be hot pressed in the panini maker at lunchtime.

I said, "Hey, Rooney, there's something I wanted to tell you."

She looked over at me. "Sure, Cammi. Shoot."

I said, "Well, you know, you probably thought I was a Mexican scholarship kid."

She didn't blink. "I never thought that."

I was surprised. "Really?"

Rooney looked back at me. "Yeah, why would I assume that?"

I said, "Well, there's a little more. My mother is actually a famous actress in Mexico City."

Rooney kept on slicing portobellos for the vegetarian Cuban sandwiches. Her knife skills were off the hook.

"I knew that too," she said.

Wait? What? "How?" I asked.

"Because I have access to the Internet, Cammi," she said. "I Googled you. You show up in the middle of the school year. You've got amazing clothes and flawless taste and clearly are not intimidated by any of this. I spoke to your father, and his English is exquisite. He sounds like British royalty. Then you wanted me to teach you how to cook, and it's clear that you're a sixteen-year-old Mexican girl who has never so much as fried a tortilla before. I figured there had to be a story there, so I Googled you."

I didn't know what to say. After a few moments of silence, I said, "Do you think the other kids know?"

Rooney looked over at me. "Do you want them to know?"

Then I did the thing that had been so hard for me for months on end: I told the truth. "I didn't before. But now, I think I should keep it real."

Rooney shrugged. "Then you're probably going to have to tell them, just like you told me. People don't tend to go looking for things they can't imagine to be true."

16

★

EAST LA

It took a while, but finally I wore Milly down and she started talking to me.

"Tell me about your mother's new role on American TV," she asked, and I didn't even mind that she asked about my mother. I'd had a nice vacation from the fame bubble.

"She plays a maid," I said. "But she's actually an entrepreneur, *nueva* Latina mogul in the making."

Milly touched her nose, then pointed to me. On the nose. "Well, my mother is a maid in real life, so if your mother protrays a stereotypical maid on TV, then you can expect me to write a letter to the studio," she said.

I nodded. Fair enough.

"So what you doing after school?"

Milly shrugged. "Homework. Lab notes for chemistry class since this crazy girl from the DF ran her mouth the whole period and I got nothing done."

I smiled. "Want to come over to my house?"

"Okay? Going to kill the lying with those two girls?"

I assured her, "The wheels are in motion."

But the truth was, that was a delaying tactic.

When we got home, my father was in the kitchen listening to the *Hamilton* sound track, which had become his obsession since we'd all gone to see the play the week before.

He was singing and rapping at the top of his lungs when I came in with Milly.

"Papá, please!" I called out. "We have company."

"It's okay," Milly said, and then quoted a line from the musical: "Immigrants get the job done!"

Then she shook my father's hand. "*Mucho gusto, Señor del Valle.*"

I could tell that my father was taken with her.

"The pleasure is all mine, young lady." They went back and forth in Spanish for a few minutes, and then my father switched back to English. "Your Spanish is so beautiful. Were you born here?"

"East LA, but Chicana through and through. You know what they say: hardly home, but always repping."

"I hear that," my father said, giving her a high five.

He even complimented her on her tattoos, even though I was fairly certain he'd never let me get inked.

I gave Milly a quick tour of the house, and she said,

"Basic BH Fab. I like it. Some of the houses are just over-the-top ostentatious."

I knew what she meant. When we were first house hunting, our Realtor, Digna, took us on an informal tour of the tackiest houses in LA. There was the house with not one but twenty-four replicas of Michelangelo's *David* sculpture on the front lawn. There was the house with a landing strip on either side of the mansion, because you know door-to-door service is what airline travel is all about. And then there was the famous party house that's used for all the OTT music videos. "That house has thirty bedrooms and fifty bathrooms," Digna said. "And I guarantee you that no matter how many times it's been cleaned, you don't want to run a black light over any of the surfaces there." Our house was nice but not cray-cray.

When we were done with our homework, I invited Milly to go for a swim in the pool, but she had to leave. "Next time," she said. "My dad works security, and he'll be getting ready for work just as my mom is getting home. I should go help make supper and take care of the little ones."

I found out that Milly had three little brothers, all under the age of ten. "I'm the oldest," she said. "Sometimes it's a pain in the butt, but those little monsters look up to me. And that's kinda cool. You know what I mean?"

I nodded, thinking of Sergio.

It had been one thing to live in Mexico without my big brother. It had been hard moving to another country without him. My bro — hardly home, but always repping.

★★★

This is the thing that any spy worth her salt can tell you—it's easy to tell a convincing lie for a couple of hours, or even a few days. But once you get into the realm of weeks and months, then you're always on the verge of getting busted.

One day I took an Uber to the Grove, and I thought I was in the clear because the driver left me in the parking lot of the natural grocery store, which was blocks away from the fancy stores where Willow and Tiggy liked to shop.

I hung back and followed along as they purchased hundreds of dollars' worth of clothes. Back in Mexico City, I used to shop like that. I didn't even have to carry cash or credit cards. The stores would let me charge whatever I wanted to my mother's account. The thing is, I never really wore most of the stuff. I'd found that it was actually more fun not to buy clothes and to "shop" in my mother's walk-in closet instead. Sure, I was tempted sometimes to buy something. Willow bought the sweetest cropped leather jacket by Alexander Wang, and it felt like my credit card was burning a hole in my pocket. I wanted so badly to whip out my card and buy my own, screaming "Twinsies!" the way I used to when Patrizia and I bought the same thing. But I knew I didn't need the jacket. It was like waking up in the middle of the night craving a cheeseburger. The feeling would pass.

We were getting smoothies at the Jamba Juice when Tiggy looked over at me and said, "Did your dad get a new job?"

"Nope," I said, slurping down my Gotta Guava smoothie.

"Really? Because I could've sworn I saw you get out of a Cadillac Escalade."

The guava drink nearly came out my nose. I had given up so many luxuries to support my little charade, but Uber Black was my weakness.

"It wasn't me," I said.

Tiggy sized me up suspiciously. "Really? Because it looked like you. My mom drove me over to Erewhon because she was out of pomegranate arils, and you know she's addicted to them."

I whipped out my monthly bus pass, which I had begun purchasing just the month before. "Must be nice," I said.

Willow looked at the bus pass. "Wow. This is expensive. Don't they have a student discount?"

I wanted to sink into the ground. Of course they probably did have a student discount bus pass. I just hadn't thought to purchase it.

"Think quickly, think quickly," I thought, tapping my foot furiously.

"If I get the student bus pass, then me and my dad can't share," I said. "This way, we save money."

Willow looked at me with her big brown eyes, and she looked as if she wanted to cry. Then she hugged me. "You make me realize how much I take for granted," she said.

Then she handed me her shopping bag. "I want you to have this," she said.

It was her Alexander Wang leather jacket.

"I couldn't," I said, and this time I meant it.

"Yes, you can," she said. "I'll ask my dad to buy me another one, and then we can be twins. Really, please, take it."

Don't hate me for what I did next. Because there are two

things you should know. Number one: it was honestly the cutest leather jacket I'd ever seen. Number two: it is rude not to accept a gift.

The next day when Sergio called to check in on me, I took a page out of my mother's telenovela play book and doused my eyes with drops so that my face would look tearstained. Then I bit my bottom lip hard before I answered Sergio's FaceTime call.

"Hey," I said listlessly.

"You don't look good," he said. "Tell me about it."

That would've been the *perfect* moment to just stop it, the lying and the pretending. But I couldn't stop. I liked the weird dichotomy of having Willow and Tiggy feel sorry for me and at the same time, the sweet superior feeling that I was getting one over on them. I wanted to keep it going, just a little longer. But I needed Sergio to think that I was a good person, not the *pendeja* he had once accused me of being. Hence the tears and the subterfuge.

"I told them," I said, lying. "And things got pretty ugly."

Sergio looked exasperated. "Well, what did you expect, *loca*? For them to throw you a parade?"

"I know, I know."

"At least you still have Milly, the friend you never lied to."

"That's true," I said. "She invited me over to her house for dinner tomorrow night."

"In East LA? You should have Albita drive you," Sergio said.

"Now who's being shallow and superficial?" I asked.

"Seriously, Cammi," he said. "LA is safer than Mexico City, but that doesn't mean you can be reckless."

I promised him I'd ask for a ride.

Of course, I had no intention of asking Albita to drive me anywhere. That Saturday, I breezed into the garden and told my parents that I was going to meet Milly at the library downtown.

My father jumped up and dangled his car keys. "No problem. I'll drive you."

Shoot. I held up my phone like it was a lightsaber. *No te preocupes, Papá.* "I can call an Uber easy peasy lemon squeezy."

My mother peered at me over her giant sunglasses, interested. "Easy greasy what?"

"Easy peasy lemon squeezy," I said slowly. "It's an expression that means 'No big deal.'"

My mother took out the little notebook where she had begun writing expressions and words that were new to her. "Say it again?"

I took the notebook from her. "I'll write it for you." I wrote it out and handed the notebook back to her.

It was cute the way she walked around with that little notebook, repeating phrases to herself like "in there like swimwear" and "it's the freakin' weekend."

My father would not be deterred. "I'm driving you, Cammi."

I gave my mother a hug and said "Your eyebrows are so on fleek" just to watch her scribble it into her notebook.

In the car, I fessed up. "Full confession, I'm not going to the library."

"I know," he said.

"I'm going over to Milly's house. She invited me for dinner."

"Sergio told me."

Only my jet-setting brother could tattle across eight time zones like that.

"So give me the address and call Milly to let her know there'll be one more for dinner."

It took nearly an hour to get to Milly's house. It wasn't that far. Just seventeen miles, but that's LA traffic for you. The minute we turned onto Whittier Boulevard, I felt like I'd been transported back to downtown Mexico City. The streets were packed with people and street vendors, colorfully decorated food trucks, and cool-looking low riders.

My father looked around, smiled, and said, "*Hombre!* It pays to go exploring. Look at that, Salazar Park."

He began to hum a song I'd never heard him sing before. Then Papá explained that Rubén Salazar was a *Los Angeles Times* reporter who died during a Vietnam War protest in 1970. Salazar had been exploring the growing resistance to the Vietnam War in the Chicano community. A songwriter composed a famous *corrido* about his death. My father whistled. "Look at this park. Swimming pool. Baseball diamond. Tennis courts. He would be proud."

If Milly and her parents hadn't been waiting for us, I think my father would've ditched me at the corner of South Alma and Whittier and gone off on an adventure.

I don't know what I expected Milly's house to be like, but I wasn't expecting Frida Kahlo's Casa Azul. Milly's house wasn't like any other on the block. It was dark blue with bright yellow shutters and had a crazy Aztec-style sculpture. The front garden was full of cactuses and other succulents. The driveway was painted like a mural with a beautiful mosaic pattern. My father whistled and said, "It's so beautiful, I don't want to drive on it."

"Hello, hello!" Milly called out as she walked onto the front porch. She showed us where to park, and then we all hugged hello.

I told her, "*Oye, chica*, you didn't mention that you lived in Willy Wonka's house."

She laughed and said, "Come and meet the Oompa Loompas."

In the backyard, three little boys jumped on and off a Slip'n Slide. Milly's mother, a pretty, petite woman who was a good three inches shorter than both of us, stood up to greet us.

"I've heard so much about you," she said. Then, peering over my shoulder, she added, "And of course, I know all about your mother's work."

"She's not here, Señora Flores," I told her. "But this is my dad."

My father did a dramatic bow and kissed the back of her hand. "*Es un placer.*"

"Hey, hey!" I heard a booming voice call out. "You've got to watch out for the slick *caballeros* from the Distrito Federal."

It was Milly's dad. He was dressed in paint-splattered

overalls and a cowboy hat. He looked cool, and I could tell as they shook hands that he and my dad would totally be friends.

"We've got pernil, rice and peas, and *aguacate*," Milly's mother said shyly.

"Yum," I said.

Milly's father clapped my dad on the shoulder and said, "Before we eat, let's talk about art. Let me show you my studio."

He took my dad into his studio, a two-car garage that he'd tricked out with a giant skylight and a fancy glass garage door. It was the kind of rolling glass door that I'd seen in my mother's design magazines. I guess, just like Willow and Tiggy did, I thought everyone who lived in East LA lived in poverty and squalor. I was embarrassed by my ignorance.

"I thought you said your dad worked security," I whispered to Milly.

"He does, but he does his night job so that he can spend his days doing what he loves—painting."

"That's cool," I said admiringly.

As I followed her to the kitchen, she said, "Let's see about those mad salad skills that you've recently acquired."

"Don't hate the player, *chica*," I reminded her. "Hate the game."

17

★

MENTIROSA

I was walking down the hallway at Polestar when I saw two teachers talking. I recognized one as Señora Sepulveda, one of the Spanish teachers in the lower school. I thought the second one might be the substitute biology teacher. Tiggy had mentioned that she was Mexican. I was walking behind them, and I heard the teacher I didn't know say, "Haven't you noticed how much Camilla looks like Carolina del Valle? They even have the same name."

My heart jumped into my throat and lodged there. I quickly darted into a doorway.

Then when I thought they were far enough ahead, I started following them again.

"They have the same last name," Señora Sepulveda

said, "but they can't be related. I heard Camilla's a scholarship kid from East LA."

"Maybe she's a poor distant cousin," the other teacher said. "Besides, if Carolina del Valle's daughter was at this school, there'd be mad security. That kidnapping madness has started to make its way across the border."

I turned then and went toward the gym, relieved that my cover wasn't blown. I was only slightly worried that kidnapping could be a danger in LA.

The fact that I was more worried about being found out than about kidnapping made me think that I had to stop telling this crazy lie. I thought, "They'll be pissed and then we'll move on." Sure Tiggy had a little bit of that RBF (resting bitch face) that Patrizia had, but she was also funny and fearless. She'd say anything to anyone, do anything if you dared her to. And Willow was the nice girlfriend I'd always wanted when I was back home. She reminded me of that beautiful human rights lawyer who married the famous actor who said he'd never get married. One day, Willow would change the world and look gorgeous doing it.

But today was not that day because they wouldn't forgive me.

There, I'd said it.

They wouldn't forgive me and I wouldn't forgive myself for blowing the kind of friendships I'd dreamed about having back at home.

All day Sunday, I rehearsed what I was going to say and how I was going to say it. There was the "It's all a big joke" approach:

"Hey, Willow and Tiggy, this is so funny. Well, you know how you thought I was poor? I'm not. And you know how you thought my mother was a maid? Well, she's not a maid; she just plays one on TV. . . ."

Then there was the "Surprise! You've been punk'd" approach:

"So, guys, I have something to confess. I've been working on a big sociological study for this AP class I've been taking at UCLA. It's all about race, class, perception, and expectation. Well, you two, you did just what we thought you'd do. Sorry for the subterfuge. Let's go to the Grove. Blue Ribbon Sushi on me."

I even played with the "Split personality" defense:

"For a very long time, I've had two personalities fighting for control over my existence. Camilla is a well-meaning and sweet but helpless pathological liar. Cammi has her feet on the ground. She is a trustworthy and upright citizen, and a good friend. You've probably met both personas over the past few months, and it's my hope that you'll forget about Camilla from the barrio and just be friends with Cammi from Beverly Hills. Okay? Are we good?"

Oddly enough, this last defense felt closest to the truth. And I began to wonder if there was any truth to what my mother had said about us being more alike than I'd thought. What I had been doing with Willow and Tiggy was acting, pretending, making up a character, and I *loved* it. But now I was ready to come clean. Sure there was bound to be some blowback, but once the truth was out, life would be so much simpler.

At school, a lot of the kids liked to joke about how elite and pampered they all were. "#firstworldproblems," they called it. Like, "My laptop is dying, but my charger is in the other room. #firstworldproblems." Or "I drove all the way to Whole Foods and they were out of my favorite Greek yogurt. #firstworldproblems." But I had managed to carve out, at least in my own twisted mind, this little loophole for myself. I was from Mexico, so I wasn't as petty and naïve as the rich LA kids I went to school with. I was an outsider at Polestar, so I knew how to keep it real. But when I looked at Milly, whose life was so much like who I was pretending to be, I knew that what I really had was #lyingtomyselfproblems.

By Monday morning, I marched into Polestar Academy with my mind on the truth and the truth on my mind. Then I sat down for lunch with Willow and Tiggy. They were going on and on about what an incredible weekend they'd had in Palm Springs.

"You guys went to Palm Springs without me?" I asked, genuinely hurt.

Tiggy explained that her mother's boutique had a pop-up shop in Palm Springs and that the family had a suite of rooms at the Viceroy and they'd invited Willow along.

"I've never been to Palm Springs," I said quietly.

Tiggy rolled her eyes. "You're from East LA. I'm assuming that there are lots of places you've never been to. Am I supposed to take you every place I go that would be a fun and new experience for you?"

Willow flinched. "Come on, Tiggy. Stop being mean."

But Tiggy was on a roll. She reached into her handbag and took out her cell phone. "Let me call my mother and tell her to book you a ticket to Paris, where we're going for spring break. I'm guessing you've never been."

It was so cold and so unexpected. I tried to cycle back through my rich-girl memories in Mexico, because Tiggy's remarks didn't just hurt my feelings. They triggered something in me, a memory of off-the-cuff remarks I'd once made in a sad attempt to seem cool or clever. I thought about all of the girls who had been my friends in fourth grade through eighth grade. I didn't know and didn't care what the parents of those girls did for a living. I assumed they had money because Greengates was an expensive school. I honestly didn't know if any of the dozen girls I'd eaten lunch with or invited over to my house had been on scholarship. We'd all worn uniforms. We'd hung out at my house because my family had had a pool and a home theater and my mother was an actress. When I thought about it, for as long as I could remember, I'd operated under the assumption that people were nice to me because of who my mother was. So I indulged them, brought them to my home, let them take selfies at the "Casa de Carolina," and I thought I was doing them a favor because they did me the favor of being my friend, letting me eat lunch with them and be part of their seemingly impenetrable circle of girls. I was so on the defensive, it never occurred to me that I might come off as aggressive or offensive, snippy or cutting in my remarks. But I bet I did. I couldn't remember what I might have said and to whom, but I was willing to bet a sizable chunk of my parents' hard-earned money that on more than a few occasions I'd been as bitchy as Tiggy was being.

I looked at Tiggy, who I'd gotten to know and like, and I could see in an instant that she was having a *pendeja* moment. I also could tell, from our months-long friendship, that she had no beloved brother like Sergio in her life—no one to tell her to rein it in and clean it up.

Willow tried to make peace. "Camilla, I'm sorry we didn't invite you to Palm Springs. I thought about it, but whenever we go, we do so much shopping and rack up the craziest room service bills. I didn't want you to feel awkward, because I know you don't have money to spend like that."

It was very, very nice of her to say. More than nice. It was a window, my opportunity to say, "Hey, guys, you went to Palm Springs without me, and yeah, that kind of stings. But the truth is, I can afford to go shopping. And oh yeah, I've been to Paris, a few times. And not to be a jerk about it, but your mother wouldn't need to book me a ticket because we usually fly private."

I could have said, "Speaking of flying private, that's how my family came to California."

I should have said, "I can't string you along any longer. My whole Cammi from the 'hood thing has been one big lie."

Instead I said, "Well, while you guys were hanging in Palm Springs, I was keeping it real in East LA."

I felt Milly standing behind me before I saw her. I turned around and tried to dial it back. Milly looked furious, like Medusa-turn-you-to-stone mad. Milly reached into her bag and handed Tiggy the copy of *People en Español* with my mother on the cover and that horrible photo of me as a kid on the inside.

"She's not poor," Milly announced. "She's not on scholarship. Her mother is one of the most famous actresses in Mexico."

"You don't live in East LA?" Tiggy asked, dumbfounded.

"No, she lives in Beverly Hills," Milly said, disgusted.

"What? That doesn't even make sense. That's not true, is it, Cammi?" Willow said.

I didn't say anything. I couldn't say anything.

"Why would you lie to us?" Willow asked. Her face was a mess of confusion, and I thought she might actually cry.

"Camilla, you see how Mexicans can be treated here," Milly said. "Instead of doing something to lift Latinos up, you make being poor and vulnerable into your own little psychodrama. You give Mexicans a bad name. *No tienes ninguna vergüenza?*" And she walked away.

Did I not have any shame? All I had was shame.

I hardly knew what to do. But I jumped up to follow Milly. Tiggy glared at me and said, "Don't leave your bag, Camilla. We don't want to be friends with you either. You're on your own."

I grabbed my bag and found Milly in the east staircase, sobbing. "You have no idea what it's like to really be Mexican in LA. My dad works security and my mother cleans houses, and about thirty-six hours a week they get to be who they are in their hearts. My father is an artist and my mother cooks up a storm for the family and plays her music and imagines herself in a *palapa* by the beach. And when the gangbangers roll through our neighborhood, shooting just to be shooting or shooting for revenge, we pray—we get down on our knees and pray—that nobody innocent gets caught in the cross fire. But there are shootings all the time—you can hear them, even if you don't dare go to your window to see what's going on. Then the next day, someone knocks on your door with a photo of a little kid—her hair is in two braids or he's got a mullet and his two front teeth are missing. And the reason they are knocking on your door is because the kid has been shot and the family doesn't have the money to buy a tiny little coffin. That's what it's like to live in East LA. It's not about pretending to be a *chola* or a *vato*. It's not about coming to a fancy school and the stupid shit that rich girls say. It's about trying to live your life in the midst of so much chaos and death. You're from Mexico City. You think you'd know better."

"I'm so sorry, Milly," I said. I was sorry, and I could feel the shame heat my skin like a fever.

"I don't get you, Camilla," she said. "You hit the jackpot in life. Crazy-talented parents. An amazing big brother. Albita is like a live-in *tía* who would lay her life down for you. You've got everything you need and everything you want. And what do you do with all that privilege? You spend months and months concocting an elaborate lie about how you're this poor kid of some hardworking maid. I'm a poor kid and my mother is a hardworking maid. All I can tell you, Camilla del Valle, is *veta a mierda*." Go to hell.

The next day we had Tapestries with Smitty, which I was dreading. I sat in a circle of my classmates, watching the candlelight glow, and all I could think was "I'm going to get my ass handed to me on a platter. I just know it."

Willow took the stick and looked directly at me. "I've been at Polestar since I was five years old. True talk, this isn't the easiest place to be biracial, half Jewish, African American identified. I got made fun of for having a permanent, albeit awesome, tan. Before I was old enough to get blow-outs on a regular basis, I got made fun of for having tight, curly hair. One of the people who is in this room, at this very moment, wrote something evil about me on the walls of the boys' bathroom. It was so mean that when my mother saw it, she cried. Then a few months ago, I met this girl from Mexico City and I thought, 'This is the kind of friend I've been waiting for, someone who gets what it's like to have a permanent, albeit awesome, tan.' I thought she was my *hermana de alma*, my soul sister."

Duncan called out, "Is this story going to take up the whole period, because I may need to take a nap or pull the fire alarm. I'm so damn bored, I could go either way."

Smitty looked over at Duncan, and Duncan stood up and said, "Why don't I save us some time and send myself to the office."

I could feel myself sweating. Not the cute beads of dew that form on your forehead when you're playing an easy game of tennis. I started to sweat like that "too long in the sauna/100 degrees in the shade/hell is hot and this might be the intro course" kinda sweat. But Willow was not done.

She continued, "It turned out that everything she told me was a lie, and it feels worse than some asshole writing racist shit about me on the bathroom wall. It makes me wonder, was I some kind of joke to this girl? Was she laughing behind my back the whole time?"

"I wasn't laughing behind your back," I blurted out.

Smitty asked, "Camilla, would you like the talking stick?"

I nodded. I stood up, and unlike the first time I held the stick, my voice wasn't trembling. I didn't feel like my bones were rattling beneath my skin. I was nervous, but damn it if I hadn't aced what Smitty had said when I'd first started at Polestar. I felt like I'd found my voice.

"I would like to apologize to Willow and Tiggy. It's true, I pretended to be something that I wasn't. But it's also true that you guys had a lot of crazy preconceptions about what it means to be Mexican. In the beginning, to tell the truth, I just rolled with it because I was curious to hear what you really thought. Sometimes you were generous because you thought I was poor and my parents were working class. But other times you were straight up racist."

Tiggy jumped to her feet and grabbed the stick, "You don't get to call me racist."

Willow stood up and took the stick from her, "As a woman of color, I reject the idea that I can even be racist."

I took the stick back from Willow and said, "That's what I used to think. But before I came to LA, I didn't even know that being Mexican made me a 'woman of color.' These labels are arbitrary, but they have a lot of power. Forget that I called either of you racist. Let's just say that we all have more power than we think. When we don't examine our assumptions about people, or when we let those assumptions slide, then we can do some serious harm—to each other and to our culture."

Smitty got to his feet and clapped. "Well said, Camilla."

Willow looked over at me as if she agreed and that she might, in the not too distant future, want to be my friend again.

Tiggy rolled her eyes and sat down next to me. As she did, she whispered, "I don't care what you say. You're still a lying bitch in my book."

★ ★ ★

In Mexico City, my mother recorded speeches for public radio, and on Octavio Paz's birthday, she did a special live performance of the Nobel Prize–winning poet's most iconic work. But in Los Angeles, where her accent was "funny," the producers were constantly sending my mother to ADR to redo her lines.

ADR stands for "automatic dialogue replacement," also known as "looping." After you film a scene, if when the director goes back to edit it, she can't hear your lines clearly, you go to an ADR studio to rerecord the dialogue. The producers then edit that into your filmed scene. My mother has no patience for this and she complains constantly.

"I spend more time looping than acting," my mother often said when we first moved to California. "Why can't they understand me? I am speaking English better than any of them can speak Spanish. I bet if you asked the average Latino viewer, they wouldn't have any trouble understanding me. I want to tell them the problem is not with my speaking, it's with your listening. It's your ears that need better, more multicultural training."

When I look back to all of my time with Willow and Tiggy, I wish I could slip into an ADR studio, dub myself, and rerecord my lines. The things I said weren't at all what I should have said, what I meant to say. I would give anything to take it all back.

18

★

THE BIG PAYBACK

Los Angeles was supposed to be a fresh start for me. I was going to get away from all of the drama of our life in Mexico, leave behind my failed friendship with Patrizia and all the damage that had been done to my mother's career as a result. Then what did I do? I came someplace new and I created new drama. I was like the troublemaker character on a telenovela whose only mission in life was to stir the pot.

I spent the rest of the day pretending to be invisible. I stared down at my notes in chem lab, the class where I'd met Milly. Every time I snuck a glance, she was staring straight ahead. Never once did I catch her eye. In the afternoon, I had Global Social Innovation with Willow. She looked over at me constantly, but every time I caught her eye, she looked devastated and then looked away. It was like I'd killed her dog.

I texted Albita to ask for a ride from school. I was almost out of the building when Tiggy cornered me at my locker.

"Just so you know, I've been suspecting you for a while," she said. She scrolled to the notes section on her phone, and there was a list of outfits I'd worn over the past few months:

March 15: Stella McCartney vest
March 27: Loewe bomber jacket
March 30: Alexander Wang track pants
April 17: Burberry trench
April 29: Fendi studded sneakers

"Your clothes are too expensive, you little liar," Tiggy snarled. "Nobody has that kind of hand-me-downs." Then she slammed her fist against my locker, which shouldn't have made me jump but it did.

As much as I didn't like Tiggy, we didn't have to be BFFs, but I knew that I didn't want an enemy. I had to make it okay.

"Make it right. Make it right," I thought. I'd screwed up, but there had to be a way to make it right. It was on me to try to get her to come around. The next day after homeroom, when I saw Willow, I handed her a shopping bag.

"What's that?" she asked.

"It's your leather jacket," I said.

"I have one," she said. "Keep it."

"But I don't deserve it," I said.

She took the bag from me, and I thought that was going to be it. Then she sniffed it.

"You keep it," she said, tossing the bag back at me. "It smells like a garbage bag full of lies."

Okay. I probably deserved that. But at least she didn't hurl the bag at me, so this might mean I still have a chance.

I did not tell Sergio about all that happened. I couldn't.

Every day at lunchtime, I hid myself away in Rooney's kitchen, but I had totally lost my touch. I put too much sriracha in the sriracha mayo. I overcooked the rice noodles for the teriyaki noodles until they were one big sticky mess. I stuck the caprese skewers in the oven and put the maple bourbon chicken skewers in the fridge.

After a week, Rooney—who was always so patient with mistakes—let me know she'd had enough.

"You're miserable," she said. "I can taste it in the food. Tell me what's up."

But I couldn't. I knew that if I told her the truth, she'd lose all respect for me. So I told her what any self-respecting teenager who doesn't want to discuss her problems says. I told her I was on drugs.

Rooney wouldn't let me off so easily. "Not actually funny, Camilla."

I'd had everything I wanted. I'd discovered that in a family full of artists and geniuses, I actually had a talent and a mentor willing to help me. I had friends who liked me (even though I lied to them), frenemies who kept me honest (Milly). And I had screwed it all up.

"Are you firing me?" I asked Rooney, even though I wasn't actually paid for my cooking services.

She shook her head. "I'm putting you on leave until you get your act together."

I nodded in agreement, blinking back the tears. It was even harder not to cry when Rooney pulled me in for a hug. "You'll be okay," she said. "It's not really high school unless you go through a little hell."

Then I ran into a bathroom stall and dialed a number I hadn't called in a long, long time.

"*Hola, Amadeo,*" I said. "*Soy yo.*"

His face popped up on my phone, as handsome and familiar as ever. We were on a break. He was my friend, not my boyfriend. But as I crouched in the bathroom stall, listening to him speak in Spanish, his voice was good medicine. He sounded like home.

★ ★ ★

Although I could've just let them leave me in the exile I so sorely deserved, I knew that I also had to try to fix things with Willow and Tiggy, at least for the sake of peace. And because I was wrong too.

Finally I got them to sit down with me. I said, "I know you're mad at me."

Willow looked at Tiggy and continued talking as if I wasn't there.

"You have every right to be mad." How to apologize without sounding like I was just defending myself wasn't easy.

Willow looked at me as if I'd committed all kinds of atrocities against small, helpless puppies, and Tiggy was doing her best "you don't exist" face.

"But this is the thing," I continued. "If I were to call up the Mexican embassy, they would agree that the two of you have said some effed-up things over the past few months."

I raced on. "You talked about how cute my accent was and you assumed that my parents were a maid and a gardener," I said.

"That's what you told us!" Tiggy burst out.

I shook my head. "Wait a minute. You liar. Don't manipulate what happened. Why would I come to a new school with the intention of lying about who I was? You threw that stuff out and I went with it, half out of curiosity about what crazy thing you might say next."

"I'm black and Jewish," Willow said. "I don't say crazy, racist *ish.*"

"Weeeeell," I began. "You behaved better than Tiggy, but not a lot better."

Willow flipped out. "You think we can agree that we're all a little racist and it will be better, but it's not. People have been talking about my skin tone, my hair, my nose, my lips, and yes, my very African American booty for as long as I can remember. I wasn't trying to put you down, Camilla. I really wanted to know what your life was like and how I could help. And yes, I did assume you were on scholarship."

I thought of the tutoring job she had created for me, the gifts, the way she'd tried to shield me from her more extravagant hangs with Tiggy. She hadn't been culturally perfect, but she really had tried. Plus, she also had to deal with prejudice and racist comments from everyone her whole life too.

Tiggy looked back and forth between us. "So now I'm the only racist one because I'm white. That's some BS."

She was so apoplectic that as she stood up she knocked her Diet Coke all over the table. She looked at it a second; then she just started to walk away.

"Tiggy," Willow called out. "You made a mess. Aren't you going to clean it up?"

Tiggy turned back and said, "Surely between the two of you, one of you is skilled enough in the fine art of housekeeping. You can do it." Then she stomped off.

Willow and I just looked at each other, stunned.

"Is she kidding?" I asked Willow.

I walked over to get some napkins to clean the mess.

"I'll help you," Willow said, grabbing some napkins too.

"Tiggy really is awful—white or pink. She's a spoiled, rich, racist brat," I muttered.

The Diet Coke had, at that point, seeped over the table and onto the floor.

"How does one can of soda make so much mess?" I wondered.

"It's Newton's law of spilled fizzy liquids. They expand in mass depending on the velocity with which they're knocked over," Willow said.

"Is that true?" I asked as we wiped off the table and the floor.

"No," Willow said. "But it sounds good, right?"

Once we'd gotten the mess cleaned up, Willow said, "Let's grab an espresso before class."

We took our cups to the common area and sat underneath a big cherry tree in bloom.

"I'm beyond pissed," Willow said. "Tiggy is mad because she hates taking on all the worst of what whiteness can imply in this country. My dad gets that way too. When some racist mess goes down, my dad is always quick to say he couldn't possibly be racist because he's a persecuted minority too. Being Jewish for him wasn't easy. Still, it's totally something else if your skin is any shade of brown. We know that."

I nodded. "I wanted Tiggy to know that plenty of what she said was out of line and she needs to stop being a rich brat."

"She knows," Willow said. "She's surrounded by people who echo back this crazy distorted rich-white-kid worldview." Willow gestured around the Polestar lunchroom. "She was just as excited as I was when we became friends with you and it was like, finally, someone who's not so cookie-cutter privileged."

"You could have been friends with Milly before I arrived," I pointed out.

"Milly never looked like she wanted to know us. We were just rich Polestar brats to her, or so we thought," Willow said. "When I saw you working in the school cafeteria, I thought, 'There is a girl who needs a friend, and God knows we need some different kinds of friends.'"

"I wasn't working, actually," I explained. "It was more like a culinary internship."

"I get that now," Willow said. "Tiggy will come back around and she'll apologize."

"She'd better," I said. "She's got some nerve and temper."

Willow paused, then said, "Pretending for five months that your mother was a maid and your dad was a gardener is nervy too."

"True that," I said, nodding.

"I gotta go," she said, and started to walk away.

"Willow! Wait up!" I was surprised to see she was no longer mad. She was crying.

I pulled her into a big bear hug. I needed one as much as she did. "Willow, I'm so sorry about all this." Much to my relief, Willow gave me a small smile.

"How about this: I'll forgive you for pretending—for five months—that your mother was a maid and your dad a gardener if you'll forgive me for being effed up and saying racist *ish*."

"Deal!" I yelled. I was so relieved. I gave her another bear hug.

"Can I ask you something?" Willow asked, as she pulled back from me.

"*Sí*, anything."

"What are you going to do with that bus pass you bought?" Willow asked as she laughed. "I can't believe you went that far, crazy," she said, incredulous. "You should donate it or something."

She was, of course, right. Donating my bus pass would be just the start.

19

★

THE DINNER PARTY

few days later, I came down to breakfast to find my father in an unexpectedly cheery mood.

"*Qué pasó?*" I asked him, breaking our English-at-home rule. Then, correcting myself, I asked, "What's up?"

He smiled. "The good news is that we have family coming to town."

I jumped up. "Sergio?"

My father nodded. I did a little victory dance. I loved our FaceTime talks, of course, but I hadn't seen Sergio since Christmas. That was before we had moved to LA. It had been just six months, but it felt like forever. Not only is Sergio coming, but everything is good with Willow. Though there was still trouble with Tiggy, and I still had to make things right with Milly, I started to feel like everything would be okay.

My father agreed that I could cook a welcome-home dinner for my big bro. I couldn't wait to go to school and ask Rooney for advice. I wanted a totally modern but really Mexican menu. She smiled when she heard my concept. "You know I'm on it," she said. The next day she handed me one of her giant index cards. I actually felt honored. The whole Polestar kitchen and menu were organized on those cards. Her handing me one meant that she was taking me seriously.

Welcome-Home-Sergio Dinner

To start
Pozole broth
with grilled shrimp, hard-boiled egg, and
ramen noodles
Then:
Sea bass à la plancha with 3 salsas: salsa
verde, salsa rojo, and jalapeño crema
Caesar salad, Tijuana style
Elotes with chili-and-lime-spiked sauce
And for dessert:
Chocolate tres leches cake with
fraises des bois

Rooney looked at me. "Do you like it? If you don't like it, I can change it."

"I like it. I love it," I said. "It just seems . . . a little above my skill set."

Rooney laughed. "If you'd like, I can come over and help?"

I nodded.

"When is this dinner?"

"Saturday night."

She said, "No problem. I'm free."

★ ★ ★

On Saturday, Rooney came over. I'd made sure we had all the ingredients needed. In no way, shape, or form was I thinking about hooking my brother up with Rooney. But from the moment she walked into our house with her curly hair falling past her shoulders, dressed in a white embroidered off-the-shoulder blouse and white jeans, it was clear that my brother was smitten.

I introduced them, and then as Rooney and I walked toward the kitchen, she whispered, "Do you think this Mexican-style blouse is too wannabe Frida Kahlo?"

"Are you kidding?" I asked. "You look amazing."

Sergio was still right behind us, and he said, "You look amazing."

Then I saw it: Rooney blushed, and I could tell. He liked her and she liked him too.

Sergio didn't want to leave the kitchen, but I kicked him out. I'd made Rooney promise to be my sous chef, handling all my prep but letting me put together each dish (with copious coaching, of course). I wanted my family to feel that I'd really made the meal for them. And now that I'd shaken off the bad mojo of my lying ways, I hoped that the food would taste of love, not stress.

When everything was nearly cooked, Rooney and I went out to the garden and decorated the outdoor table with one of my mother's favorite tablecloths. Rooney had brought along a bag of rose petals that she'd gotten at the flower market downtown. We sprinkled those on the table, setting each place with simple white dishes and leaving plenty of room for the food.

Once everything was on the table, we called everyone to the garden. Sergio took the lead in introducing Rooney, while I poured everyone drinks from a big pitcher of guava agua fresca.

The looks on my parents' faces made the hours in the kitchen so worth it. They walked out the back patio door as if they were lottery winners being escorted to their prize.

"You did this?" my mother asked, wrapping her arms around me. "All of this?"

"Well, Rooney helped," I said, beaming at her.

"Very impressive, both of you," my father said, raising his glass in a toast. "To our son, who has come home. To Rooney, a new friend. And to our daughter, who against all odds has learned to cook."

Everyone laughed.

After the toast, Rooney gave me a hug and urged everyone to sit down and eat.

My parents oohed and aahed over every course, though I think the pozole with the ramen noodles was probably their favorite. The only thing that interested Sergio more than

Rooney was the chocolate cake. He kept talking to her in French, and it turned out that Rooney had spent a summer interning in Lausanne, Switzerland, where Sergio went to school. By the time the meal was over, my parents had taken their coffee into the media room. I went into the kitchen to clean up, and Rooney and Sergio stayed outside in the backyard until very, very late. I could not imagine a better way to welcome my bro into our new home.

As for me, when I got up to my room, I picked up my phone, and immediately I knew who to call. I hit a phone number that was so familiar to me that I didn't need speed dial to remember all the numbers, I knew. I was missing my hometown doctor, Amadeo. He was not close, but he was just a four-hour flight away. Amadeo. I loved the me I was when I was with him. I was tired of being on a break.

"*Hola, Amadeo,*" I whispered into the phone, as if I was in a crowded theater and not alone in my bedroom. "*Soy yo.*"

20

★

THE BLOCK PARTY

I didn't know how I was going to make up for all the lies I'd told, but I knew that I needed to do more than apologize. As Rooney often said, "I'm not a Buddhist, but I believe in karma. What goes around comes around." I needed and wanted something good to come my way—even if it was just the feeling that I could look in the mirror and not think, "Ay, Cammi, no" or "Ay, Cammi, why?" every day of the week.

Willow and I made our peace pretty quickly. I think out of all of us, she and I had the most in common. I wasn't mixed the way she was, but I had one foot in my life in Mexico and one foot in LA and it was that particular mix that I'd found so hard to navigate. Tiggy kept insisting that we wanted to blame her for "everything" because she was white. Finally, one day after school, the three of us met up at the Grove and Willow put her foot down.

We were sitting in a booth at Blue Ribbon Sushi, our old stomping grounds. We had just ordered and we were sipping tiny cups of green tea because even though it was California, and it was hot outside, the air-conditioning was on full blast. Willow and I sat on one side of the booth, Tiggy sat on the other.

She said, "I'm still not speaking to her. She's a liar."

Willow put her tea cup down and said, "Yep, that's been established. But we're not here to talk about Cammi, we're here to talk about you. You've done some ra— Let's not call it racist. Mad culturally insensitive ish and you've got to fix it. You can start by apologizing for spilling the Diet Coke and expecting us to clean it up."

Tiggy looked genuinely embarrassed.

"What?" I said. "You thought we'd just forget about that?"

"I'm sorry," she said, not arguing, but looking more at Willow than at me. "That was out of line."

It was so obvious that Tiggy had never had to apologize for anything in her life. This looked like the harshest thing she's ever had to do. As much as I hate to admit it, I felt a little sorry for her. Willow was a little less forgiving.

"I didn't mean it. I was just so angry, and I felt left out, seeing you two band up together after everything she did." I stopped feeling sorry for her immediately. "And I know it's not an excuse, but I snapped. I lashed out."

"Okay, am I supposed to feel bad for you because you suffer from white fragility?" Willow responded. I had to give her props, that was definitely the right term to use here.

"Willow, I'm so sorry. You're my best friend," Tiggy pleaded with her. "I need you, please . . . you're right. I'm f***d up, I'm . . . racist, okay?"

That looked really hard for her to say.

"But I'm working on it, I swear," she added.

"You've been out of line and all over the place for a while, Tiggy," Willow said. "Do you even want to be our friend anymore?"

Tiggy shrugged, "I want to be your friend, Willow. Things were so much easier before she came around."

Willow shook her head. "Easier for you, maybe, but not easier for me. I like not being the only person of color in our squad. I like having a different perspective in the mix. It's what our whole school is supposed to be about."

Tiggy scowled, "But she's not even really poor."

"But I am really Mexican," I said. "And even though I lied about what my parents do for a living, the way I feel about things as a Mexican hasn't changed."

"So what do you say, Tiggy?" Willow asked. "Are you down with the rainbow tribe?"

"Sure," Tiggy said. Then she nodded in my direction. "As long as the rich girl pays for lunch."

I took out my black card and put it on the table. "Done."

Tiggy looked at me and shook her head. "I knew that card was real. Positive thinking, my booty."

Making up with Milly was harder. No matter how many times I approached her at school, she just shut me down. Every time I tried to pass her a note in class or give her one at her locker, she made a big show of ripping it up. Then finally, one day I decided to FedEx a letter to her house. I thought maybe if she got an overnight package that someone had to sign for, she would at least read it before she ripped it up.

In the letter, I wrote:

> Dear Milly,
>
> I get it. I screwed up. I disrespected you and I disrespected myself by playing into other people's beliefs about our culture. Would it help if I explained that I'm new to this country and that English isn't my first language? (Ha, ha.) But really, the thing is, I didn't know before I moved to Los Angeles just how deep the misconceptions were about us Mexicans, just how damaging the stereotypes could be. So I'd like to apologize for that.
>
> My father always told me and Sergio that it's okay to fail, as long as we failed forward. If we learned something, if we could then use what we learned, then the failure was worth it. I've learned a lot in the past few months. I'm trying to use what I've learned.

*I can't beg you to be my friend. I can say
that you're someone who I'd like to continue
to hang with. You make me proud to be
Mexican. I think together we can do a lot of
good and maybe even have some fun. But
regardless, I hope you'll accept my apology.*

Sinceramente,
Camilla

I sent the letter on Friday for Saturday delivery. All day Saturday and into Sunday, I kept checking my phone for a text and I had to resist the urge to text her. Just the act of writing the letter made me realize that I couldn't make Milly be my friend. The way she iced me out made me think of all my elementary school friends I'd cut off, just because they asked my mom for an autograph. Yeah, I was a kid. But until it happened to me, I didn't realize how much it hurt to have made a mistake with someone and not be given a chance to fix it.

That Monday in chemistry, I walked into the classroom to see Milly sitting at her desk. She had a Bunsen burner and my letter, which she proceeded to torch. I looked at her in disbelief. I didn't think she could've found another way to tell me to screw myself, but I had to give her props. She was crazy creative.

When she was done, she walked over to me and poured the ashes on my desk.

"Wow, thanks," I said, sarcastically.

"Talk is cheap," she said. "Let's see what you do."

"Okay . . . ," I said.

"My Dad misses hanging with your Dad," she said. "He wants me to invite your father to lunch on Saturday. You can come."

Milly and I were sitting on the sidewalk in front of her house when I had the biggest brainstorm. She said, "When I was a kid, we used to have the best block parties every summer."

I'd never heard of a block party, but Milly explained, "We'd close the street down to traffic. There'd be a bouncy house for the little kids, music, dancing, all this food. It was great."

I nodded. "It sounds like the street festivals in Coyoacán. I love that kind of thing."

"Me too," Milly said. "But we don't have them anymore."

"Why not?"

"All the old ladies who used to plan them either passed away or moved away. It's a ton of work. You've got to fundraise, get permits from the city to close the streets, hire people, organize everything."

I jumped up. "I can do it. I can be that old-lady organizer."

Milly shook her head. "You know you're crazy, right?"

On the way home, I talked to my dad and he agreed to help me. He'd just finished his big voice-over project, so both he and Rogelio were free. Every day after school, we had meetings at our house. I'd been working on my friendships for days, trying to make sure Willow and Tiggy didn't hold a grudge. Milly had been to our house, but true talk, it was weird the first time Willow and Tiggy came over.

"You've got to be kidding me," Tiggy said when I opened the front door.

"This is niiiiiice," Willow said. "And I know nice."

A few weeks later, it had all come together. We called our block party "Coyoacán Comes to East LA," and early one Saturday morning, we all drove to Milly's block. And by "early" I mean five a.m. There was so much to do. Rooney got a few friends who had food trucks to roll through. All the food was free because my parents had agreed to underwrite the whole thing. By seven a.m., the street smelled like heaven—there was Korean barbecue grilling away, a Hawaiian poke bowl truck, and, of course, two taco trucks serving the best of Mexican street food.

There was a bouncy house. Because Milly had insisted. "Nostalgia, man," she said, trying to pretend she wasn't all sentimental about it. "That ish runs deep."

Tiggy and her mother organized a street-style fashion show using guys and girls from the community, and they were all set up to broadcast it live on teenvogue.com.

Milly's dad gave painting lessons, and my mom took selfies with fans next to the free photo booth that we had set up.

The costume designers from my mother's TV show had

set up a huge tag sale of clothes, handbags, and shoes from the shows they had worked on, things that weren't needed for the next television season. Everything was being sold supercheap. All the proceeds were going to the Polestar scholarship fund.

Speaking of which, we got the Admissions Department to set up a table so that kids from Milly's neighborhood could learn about opportunities and even apply. There was also a raffle so that five kids could get free admission to Polestar's summer day camp. I looked at all the kids lined up to meet the admissions counselors. The girls and boys looked like they could have been the little brothers or sisters of me and Sergio, or of Willow, or of Milly. At one point Milly, Willow, and I just stood there looking at the kids.

Milly wiped a tear that had gotten away from her and said, "*Sin palabras.*"

I said, "Exactly."

Willow asked, "What does that mean?"

I explained that it's a phrase that means "Words aren't necessary."

And Willow said, "*Sí, hermanas.* I agree."

She was cute like that.

At the end of the afternoon, the band started to play. My father had found musicians in Salazar Park and hired them to be our headliners, and they played old-style Latin music. My mother was dressed down, in a simple sundress and a simple ponytail. But she was also wearing a pair of impossible heels because, you know, that's how she rolls.

When the music started to play, she came over to me and said, "I'm very proud of you, Camilla. I probably don't say that enough. You're like your dad. You've got a lot of heart."

Then she went over to my father and said, "*Oye, Viejo,* want to dance?"

For a little while, it was just the two of them, in the middle of this street in East LA, twirling and dancing. But soon others started to join them. When the band started to play an old reggaeton song, me and my crew started dancing too. Willow and Milly were the best dancers. They looked like they had just come off tour with Beyoncé. But Tiggy and I did our best to keep up, collapsing into giggles every time we tried to execute one of their more complicated moves.

I knew it would take a while for my new friends to trust me again, but for the first time since it had all gone south, I began to feel that I was a person worthy of that trust.

Late that night the band was still playing, and the kids, hopped up on sugar, were still crawling all over the bouncy house. Families had set up folding chairs on the street, and they drank cerveza and big cups of Cuban coffee, and talked animatedly, with their arms flailing about this, that, and everything. My girls and I were exhausted, so we lay out on Milly's painted driveway. It would be summer soon, and we all had different plans.

"Where are you off to?" I asked Willow.

"New York," she said. "I got an internship at the Jewish Museum. They're doing some black and Jewish exhibit."

Milly, who loved all kinds of art, said, "That sounds mad cool."

Tiggy shook her head. "It sounds weird. You're not even that into being Jewish, but that's pretty cool."

Willow shrugged. "Culture is everything, so it should be interesting, I hope."

Tiggy said, "My parents have rented a house in the Hamptons. You can come visit us when you get bored. I mean, if you get bored."

"I definitely will," Willow said. "How about you, Milly?"

Milly smiled. "I'm going to Rock Camp this summer. I'm going to learn how to play guitar. Write a few songs. Rock out."

I smiled. "That sounds like fun."

"What are you going to do, Cammi?" Willow asked.

"I'm going back to Mexico," I said, beaming. "My mother has to stay here and shoot her show, but Rooney has the summer off, and she and Sergio are going to work on this soccer thing. My dad's coming too."

"That sounds cool," Milly said.

"And I want to see my boyfriend," I added.

Everyone looked shocked.

"You have a boyfriend?" Willow asked.

"Yeah," I said with a goofy smile. "His name is Amadeo and he's in medical school."

Now Tiggy was interested. "You have an *older* boyfriend, in medical school? Then why were you all infatuated with white Max?"

"Amadeo and I were on a break," I began sheepishly.

"Your idea or his idea?" Willow asked.

"My stupid idea," I confessed.

Milly said, "Let's see a picture of him."

I pulled up a photo on my phone and handed it to her.

She whistled. "He is devastatingly handsome. Only a fool would take a break from a hottie like this."

What could I say? It was pretty well established that wise decisions had not been my forte lately. I was happy that I'd be back at Polestar in the fall, but I couldn't wait to get home—back to my guy and the girl I used to be.

21

★

THE BACK NINE

My mother's show in the US was a huge hit, and just as she'd suspected, the studio had ordered the back nine before the first episode had even aired. Things were a little bit back to normal as we had known it in Mexico City. There were photographers waiting outside our house every day, and my mom began to travel with a driver who doubled as security. One Saturday afternoon, the two of us were swimming in the pool, protected from the prying eyes of the paparazzi not only by a good fence but by a row of English-style hedges. "I miss my anonymity," she said. "It was fun to be un-famous for a while." I nodded, but noted the key words "for a while."

"I'm very proud of you," I told her. "You are a star in two

languages and many countries. How many people can say that?"

"*Gracias!*" she said, wrapping me in her arms. "How about when the show goes on hiatus, you and me take a girls' trip to a spa?"

"Sure," I said. I sensed that the puzzle piece that was my mother would continue to be a tricky one. My mother was so big and so bright, and I had to share her with the world. But as I swam laps with her in the pool, our favorite Låpsley album wafted like stardust from the backyard stereo system. I realized what a gift it was to have these moments when I had my mother all to myself. She was, first and foremost, my mother. I wondered if my relationship with her would benefit if I could create a space where she could enter my life as Mamá first and actress second.

Despite the fact that I'd spent a good part of my first year in the US being a complete *pendeja*, I'd actually learned a few things. I'd learned that being from another country— even one with a financial safety net—is like having all the pieces of your life cut into shapes that are entirely unfamiliar to you. Your job, as a New American, is to put the pieces together. No one gets to carry his or her puzzle whole across the border. You cannot keep being the same person you were in that other place. The very act of migration throws all of the pieces into the air. Up there, high above any place you can easily reach, the pieces are scrambled with elements you can't always divine or control—language, geography, race, class, and opportunity. There are X factors that play a role, things like luck and friendship, support and love (which is another kind of luck). The pieces come back to you, sometimes so quickly that they knock you over with their strength and speed. Sometimes it feels like a piece of you—a piece that you knew, loved, and treasured back home—is lost forever. You wait for it, patiently at first, and then impatiently. There's a hole in your heart where this piece belongs, and if the piece does not return, you must carefully search for a new one to take its place.

By the end of my school year, I had enough of the pieces that I could recognize myself, even though I knew I was changing. It's like what my dad told me when he first taught me how to do puzzles—if you can find the corners, you will eventually be able to fill in the rest.

I had four corners. In the upper left, there was my heart, my North Star—my brother, Sergio. I couldn't wait to spend the summer with him in Mexico. It would be good to be home.

In the upper right, I had Milly. She was my *hermanita* homegirl, my sister from another mister. I never would've thought that all the drama could make us closer, but it did. And now that I knew what it was like to not have Milly's friendship, I treasured it even more.

I wouldn't have guessed when I first met Willow and Tiggy that they would make up one of my American puzzle corners, but they did. We were so different—all three of us—but in our differences, talking-stick style, we had created this connection built on a foundation of curiosity, affection, and respect.

My fourth corner was Rooney. In addition to being an

amazing chef, she was also a total soccer geek. As my brother put it, she was "the perfect woman." On any given Saturday, I could find Rooney and Sergio—home for the summer—on the sofa watching soccer and drinking Mexican Coke. Rooney had heard about this social innovation soccer ball that these college girls had invented. Kids play with this soccer ball all day, and while they play, the ball collects kinetic energy. Then at night, the ball can be connected to a lamp for the kids to do homework. It even has a night-light setting. Rooney and Sergio were going to Mexico City at the end of the summer with a thousand balls to give out to kids in the city's poorest neighborhoods. I was going with them. I couldn't wait to show my friend and mentor my hometown.

Back home in Mexico, I'd always had this idea that I would go to college and study art history. But the longer I stayed at Polestar, the more I began to believe that the path for me was anything but clear. I didn't need to pick one topic and one safe place where a good girl from a good family could forge a career. My mother once told me that the beauty of telenovelas was their over-the-top grandiosity. "Our novelas show the world as this crazy place where anything can happen. Our viewers, both the women and the men, love us for the romance, the luxurious settings, the houses, the cars, the clothes. But what really speaks to them, what wraps our stories around their hearts, is the sense of possibility. Novelas are fairy tales. They show us that there should not be ceilings on our dreams."

I was beginning to think that Polestar—despite all the lies I'd told, or maybe in part because of them—was my novela. It was the place that had helped me lift the ceiling off my dreams.

And no teacher had helped me see life differently more than Mr. Agrabal. One Friday afternoon, after Mr. Agrabal had shown us a Bollywood movie, I stayed after class. I explained to him that my mother was an actress and that in Mexico she had starred in these television series called telenovelas. I explained that the novelas reminded me of Bollywood films. I asked him if the following Friday I could stay after school and show him one of my mother's telenovelas. He said he would love to see it. He also said I could invite a few friends.

When the big day arrived, Mr. Agrabal was dressed to the nines in a mint-green suit with a crisp white shirt and a khaki tie. I'd debated about which film to bring and had decided finally on the *romance histórico, Mundos sin Fronteras*, my mother's first novela. I was joined by Tiggy, Willow, and Milly. I invited Smitty too, because while he took a lot of guff for his class and the whole Native American council vibe, I liked Tapestries. It had given me a chance to say what I'd needed to say, and to offer apologies when I'd totally screwed up.

Mr. Agrabal had just lowered the shades and pulled down the screen when my father arrived.

"Am I late?" he asked innocently, as if he'd shown up for a tailgate party in the parking lot of a football stadium.

He held up a small cooler. "I brought Mexican colas."

We had just started the first episode of *Mundos sin Fronteras* when we heard a knock at the door.

"Did somebody order popcorn?"

I heard her before I saw her. It was my mother, and she rolled in one of those old-fashioned popcorn machines. A gift, she explained, for a true film fan, Mr. Agrabal.

When she went over to introduce herself to my chem teacher, I thought he might faint. "You are so beautiful," he said, kissing her on the hand.

"I take after my daughter," she said, winking at me.

I hugged her and thanked her for stopping by.

"I am not stopping by," she said. "I was able to change my shoot schedule. I am staying."

"Where do you sit?" she asked, and I showed her. She sat down in my classroom seat. My father sat next to her and grasped her hand.

"Hey! No making out!" Tiggy teased.

"Yeah, keep it clean," Willow added.

Then Mr. Agrabal dimmed the lights and the series began. Rose after rose opened up, bloomed, and then fell away, until finally the action began. There was my mother, both on-screen and in real life. In real life she was holding on to my father, who I loved more than I loved myself. On-screen my mother was just eighteen years old. She was just a couple of years older than I was. She would make mistakes. She did not have all the answers. But she was confident that she would find her way. Everything, I mean *everything*, was just beginning. I wasn't in a telenovela, but for the first time, as I watched my mother on the screen, I thought I knew exactly how she must have felt. For me, things were just beginning too.

AUTHOR'S NOTE

In *The Go-Between,* my goal is to tell a story that every first-generation American knows well. It is a story about remembrance and reinvention that gets to the heart of the questions every immigrant family must wrestle with: Who were we *back there?* Who are we *here?* Who does everyone *think* we are here? Who might we become here, under the best of circumstances and the worst of circumstances? And how do we meld all those selves together in a way that is graceful and seamless?

I've used the word *immigrant* in its broadest sense, because Camilla's family had a home they could return to. I was born in Panama and lived my early childhood in Northern England, then moved to the US when I was five. Throughout my childhood, it seemed that every personal introduction had a story, and sometimes a story underneath that story. *This is Juan, who is your father's cousin's husband. He had another family in Nicaragua. Those children don't live here. This is Belén, who does hair. But in Panama, she was a nurse and her father was a doctor.*

In this book, I'm drawing from the worlds—television, Los Angeles, first-generation teenagers—I know well. Not everyone has parents who are actors, but I think the themes are universal: one parent working, one parent not working and the tensions therein; class differences between close friends; and the gulf between who you were at one school and who you are perceived as being at a new school.

I wanted to write a book in which the heroine was Latina, but not working class. I felt that it was important, not just as a fantasy, but as a representation of the spectrum of reality. I didn't grow up enjoying wealth like Camilla's, but her story does reflect the lives of privilege of Latinas I know and love. It felt almost more dangerous to play with class than it did to take on issues of race. I grew up in hip-hop culture, where "keeping it real" is the ultimate compliment. But I think, as Camilla learns, you don't have to be poor to keep it real. And conversely, the struggle for a sense of self and place for Latinas in this country is real, regardless of your wealth or class.

My main character has a mother who plays a maid on TV. This choice was directly related to the famous comment made by the first black Oscar winner, Hattie McDaniel, that she would rather play a maid than be one.

The challenges of the main characters in *The Go-Between* speak to how everyone seeks to find their own place, and while Camilla's circumstances are extraordinary—her mom is a telenovela actress, after all—all the teens in the book are on a similar path, trying to work with what they've been given while trying to make sense of what it means to grow up and find your place in the world.

I hope that teen readers of all backgrounds find that Camilla's journey of "faking it until you figure it out" is one that feels both fresh and familiar.

ACKNOWLEDGMENTS

I am so grateful to my mother, Cecilia Ortega, for braving the unknown and bringing me to America, and to my step-father, Antonio Ortega, for his encouragement and support. Beverly Horowitz is the best editor a girl could hope for, and I'm grateful to Rebecca Gudelis for answering a gazillion emails that said "Just a few more days" with aplomb. Thanks as well to Kimberly Witherspoon, Monika Drake, and the whole Inkwell team.

Gracias a mi Aunt Diana and Uncle Buster for always believing and to my *prima hermana* Digna as well. Jason Clampet makes me laugh and brings me empanadas. Thank you to Jerry and Mary Clampet for Flora care so I can write. Isabel Rivera and Mai El-Khoury are good friends who understand my immigrant heart. Flora already knows that *cada verano tiene su historia*. *Querida*, this one's for you.

ABOUT THE AUTHOR

Veronica Chambers is a prolific author, best known for her critically acclaimed memoir, *Mama's Girl*. Most recently she was the editor of as well as a contributor to *The Meaning of Michelle: 16 Writers on the Iconic First Lady and How Her Journey Inspires Our Own*. She has written more than a dozen books for young readers, including *Plus* and the Amigas series, and has cowritten *New York Times* bestselling adult memoirs with Robin Roberts, Eric Ripert, Michael Strahan, and Marcus Samuelsson. She was cowriter as well on Samuelsson's young adult memoir, *Make It Messy*.

Veronica lives with her husband and daughter in Hoboken, New Jersey. Visit her online at veronicachambers.com and follow her on Twitter at @vvchambers.